TIME RUNNERS
WIPE OUT

JUSTIN RICHARDS

SIMON AND SCHUSTER

SIMON AND SCHUSTER
First published in Great Britain by Simon and Schuster UK Ltd, 2008
A CBS COMPANY

1 3 5 7 9 10 8 6 4 2

Simon & Schuster UK Ltd
Africa House
64–78 Kingsway
London WC2B 6AH

A CIP catalogue record for this book is
available from the British Library

ISBN 13: 978-1-41692-645-0

Typset by Rowland Phototypesetting Ltd,
Bury St Edmunds, Suffolk
Printed and bound in Great Britain by
Cox & Wyman Ltd, Reading, Berks

For JAC and Kate – Runners in waiting

CHAPTER ONE

⏱ SUNDAY 11TH SEPTEMBER 1955

It didn't look like the sort of house where the end of the world would start. And that was fine, because Anna and I hadn't planned on doing any 'end of the world' stuff. Though as things turned out, it wasn't really up to us.

But, as so often with time travel, I'm getting ahead of myself. It was a house – just a plain, ordinary large house in its own small grounds within easy reach of London. When Senex sent us here, he'd told Anna she was going home. Senex is the man who's in charge of me and Anna. He decides where we're needed, where there's a problem with time that we can sort out.

1

We've stopped a man with a sniper rifle in Shakespearean England, and a sabre-toothed tiger at my school. That's what we do – we're Time Runners. We sort out problems with time – fix it when it goes wrong.

Oh, and we don't exist. But you of all people should know that by now. I fell through a time break – that's a sort of hole in time – and was lost. It's as if I never existed. There never was a boy called Jamie Grant. I never went to my school, my sister never had a brother, my parents never had a son.

The same sort of thing happened to Anna, though a long time before it happened to me. That was what Senex meant when he said she was going home. He didn't mean a place – he meant a time. And the time he meant was 1955. The year Anna was lost. The year when time finally realised there was no such person and a fifteen-year-old girl flicked out of existence in the blink of an eye. Not my eye or Anna's, obviously – because, as I said, we don't exist.

'Why are we here?' I wondered out loud as we stood in the driveway and looked at the house.

It was squarish, made of stone that was lightish, and it looked, well, pretty ordinary-ish really. The sun was dipping down behind the trees and the shadows were long across the drive. Time was standing still.

'I mean,' I went on, 'I'm sure it's a great year and you've probably got loads of memories. But – why?'

'Senex was a bit vague,' Anna agreed. 'Time break. Dinner party. Something wrong.'

'Go and investigate. And if it's easy, fix it.'

'If it isn't, send for help.'

Like I said, the end of the world wasn't really on the agenda at that stage.

The dinner party was at eight o'clock. We didn't know if that was important – maybe one or more of the guests would cause a problem. A problem with time. Or maybe it would be something completely different. But Anna couldn't detect anything untoward yet and it all felt OK to me. I can sort of tell when there's a problem. Maybe 'OK' is too strong – I wasn't sure that everything was fine, but I didn't get the feeling I do when there's big trouble. That's like nausea, like being punched in the stomach, like – well, you know it when you feel it.

'Wait till eight?' I suggested.

'You can wait if you like,' Anna said. She's got a sort of half-smile when she's teasing. 'I'm going straight there.'

'Let's make it a few minutes before,' I suggested. 'Then we can have a mooch round first.'

'A mooch round?' She was adjusting a thing that looked like a wristwatch. It wasn't a wristwatch.

'Explore, investigate, case the joint. You know.'

'I know.'

'Ten to eight, then?'

Anna nodded. 'Ladies first,' she joked.

'Age before beauty,' I said.

She laughed. 'I'm old enough to be your mother.' She's right. More than right. She might look only a few years older than me at the most, but she was born in 1940.

'That's what I meant,' I told her.

We set our time dials and the world started up

again. Shadows lengthened, the sun disappeared. Lights came on in the windows of the house and it was ten to eight. Suddenly. Just like that. In a moment.

Then time was still once more. We walked up the driveway to the house, our feet not crunching on the time-locked gravel. There was a car outside the house – boxy and black. A driver was frozen in position as he stood by the back door, hand on the handle, about to open it. In the darkness we couldn't see who was inside.

'Let's explore,' Anna said. She was looking slightly odd and I could hear a tension in her voice.

'Yes, let's,' I agreed. 'Are you OK?'

'Course I am,' she snapped.

'Good,' I said quickly. 'Because I think you're OK. Not edgy or anything. Oh no.'

She didn't answer and I followed her up the short flight of stone steps that led to the front door. I could feel the time beneath my feet, sense it pouring out of the stonework of the house. If I let it register I would know the age of every component – when each stone was positioned and even when it was formed, millions of years ago. It's like background noise in a crowded room. You have to filter it out and just listen to the useful, interesting, relevant bits. Otherwise you'd go bonkers.

'So, what are we looking for?' I asked as we stood in the entrance hall. It was a wide, marble-floored area. There was a grandfather clock frozen at ten to eight. (Made in 1873, from wood that came from a tree that was 148 years old when it was cut down – 148 years, three months and eleven days if you want to know exactly. I don't need to count the rings.)

'I'm not sure really. Just anything that's – you know – *wrong.*'

'We could always ask,' I suggested.

As well as the grandfather clock (and a table with a telephone on it), there was a man standing just inside the front door.

'Gerald Chowdry,' Anna said. 'He owns the house. Lives here with his wife, Diane.'

He was a tall man, slightly stooped, with grey hair and wire-framed glasses. 'Fifty-six years old, give or take a month or two,' I said.

'Works in Whitehall. Civil servant,' Anna went on, taking up the man's story. 'In the War Office. Quite senior, and well respected.'

We'd been reading up on them in the library. Not just any library, mind – the Library at the End of Time. You can find out anything there, about anyone. But you can't predict what's going to go wrong with time itself – if you read about that it's too late, because it's already happened.

'And tonight the Chowdrys have guests for dinner,' I said.

'And something will take place that isn't supposed to happen.'

'Question is, what?'

From looking at the floor plans I knew that a study and a drawing room came off the hall, then further along was the dining room. A narrow passageway led down to the kitchen and access to the servants' quarters. A wide staircase swept up to the bedrooms and bathrooms above.

The table settings told us that there would be five for dinner. Or at least, five were expected. In the kitchen we found the cook and a maid, who presumably would also have to serve. The cook was caught in the moment of licking soup off her finger, which I didn't think was a terribly good sign really.

Diane Chowdry was halfway down the stairs, one foot frozen in mid-step as she descended. She was small and mousy, her hair very obviously dyed and pinned up severely. She was wearing a rather shapeless print dress and a necklace of small pearls. She also wore a diamond brooch, but I could tell at a glance the exact origins of the glass the 'diamond' had been cut from.

'So far, so boring,' I said, heading up the stairs past Mrs Chowdry.

And then I saw the ghost.

At the top of the stairs there was a wide landing, then a corridor leading to the bedrooms. A large window gave out to the front of the house. I could see a car parked on the drive below, illuminated by the outside light and with the driver still frozen at the point of opening the back door for his passenger.

Because it was mostly dark outside, the window reflected the view of the landing behind me. Movement drew my eye and I could see Anna further down the corridor. But she looked different somehow – her hair was all over the place, and she was wearing a different dress.

And she was screaming.

Silently screaming. She seemed to be moving in slow motion, her long hair in a frenzy as she shook her head and struggled to pull free from . . . something.

I spun round. And the real Anna was right beside me. Smiling.

'What is it?' she asked.

I couldn't answer. I just pointed down the corridor.

Where Anna – the other Anna – was still screaming and struggling, silent and in slow motion. The air around her was an unfocused blur. Beside-me-Anna gasped.

'Skitters,' she said.

I could see them then. The blurs and movements round the girl who wasn't Anna – who couldn't be Anna, could she? – resolved themselves into shapes. Creatures. Like gargoyles or imps. Skitters are nasty, mischievous creatures that live outside time as we know it. They're always up to no good and you can't really see them unless, like Anna and me, you're outside time too. But you might catch the odd glimpse. See a movement out of the corner of your eye, a blur of motion where there isn't anything, a hint of reflected movement in a mirror or a puddle . . . That could be a Skitter.

The Skitters had got hold of the girl – of Anna – and were dragging her backwards along the corridor. She fought and yelled and tried to break free, but they held her tight.

'What's happening?' Anna said.

She took a step towards the reflected version of herself, but I caught her hand and held her back. 'I don't know. I'm not getting anything. It's like they aren't really there.'

'I'm a ghost?' she breathed.

'Or an echo, or a might-yet-be, or . . .' I shook my head. 'I don't know. I'm sorry,' I added, seeing how pale she now was.

Anna's ghost, or whatever it was, had become translucent. It was fading away as we watched. The Skitters had dragged her to one of the doors along the corridor. The third door on the right-hand side. She managed to wrench her arm free, reaching back towards us – though she couldn't know we were there – fingers clutching the air. Then a stone-faced Skitter snatched it back and the creatures hurled ghost-Anna at the door.

She faded as she reached it. Or maybe, being a ghost, she went through the door.

I was still clutching Anna's hand – *my* Anna's hand. She was holding on tight in fear and confusion.

The only sound was the deep, steady ticking of the grandfather clock in the hall below.

Anna sensed it as soon as I did. 'Time,' she said. 'I didn't – did you?'

I shook my head as Diane Chowdry continued down the stairs, calling to her husband.

Time had started up again. Anna and I both turned and looked over the rail at the top of the stairs, down into the hall.

'Mr Lewis is getting changed for dinner,' Diane Chowdry announced. 'Though why you had to invite him, I don't know.'

'I told you, I didn't,' her husband insisted. 'Blessed fellow's a law unto himself. Invited himself along tonight, just as he invited himself to come and work in the office so far as I can tell. No idea what his real job is. He just turned up last Thursday, out of the blue – "Hello, I'm here to help." Got a nerve, though.'

'He has indeed.'

She was in the hall now. Outside a car door slammed shut.

'What about the other fellow?' Gerald Chowdry was asking his wife. 'Your chap – what's his name? The invalid.'

'Oh, I doubt we'll see Mr Prophecy. He's in his room and mustn't be disturbed.'

'Third on the right, I know.'

Anna gripped my hand tighter. 'That's the room where –'

'Yes,' I whispered. I was all too aware that with time running normally now – however that had happened – the Chowdrys, and everyone else, could see us.

This included the young man with slicked-back dark hair and wearing a suit who stepped out of a room on the left of the corridor and hurried towards the landing.

'Hello there,' he said loudly. 'I'm Mark Lewis. And who might you be?'

In the hall below, the Chowdrys looked up at us. Gerald frowned. His wife's face was filled with surprise.

Before I could say anything, another man stepped into the hall, the front door swinging shut behind him. The man from the car. He too looked up at us and I could see he was middle-aged. A tall, well-built man with a rugged face and thinning fair hair. There was something about him that made me feel I could trust him – some instinct in among the wealth of information about his age, how old his suit was, when he had last shaved, had his hair cut, grew his first adult tooth . . . He smiled and nodded, reminding me vaguely of someone, though he showed no sense of recognition. Then he turned his attention to Gerald Chowdry and his wife.

Beside me Anna was staring open-mouthed down into the hallway at the man shaking hands with Gerald Chowdry, the man introducing

himself to Mrs Chowdry: 'Colin Preston. From
Whitehall.'

'Dad?!' Anna said.

CHAPTER TWO

I suppose the sensible thing would have been to stop time again. But I wasn't really sure why or how it had started up. And sensible isn't always the first thought in my head. Especially with Anna almost fainting in surprise and staring at her father – the father who never knew she existed. Not any more.

Everything was happening in a bit of a rush. I did have my finger ready on the time dial, prepared for a speedy escape if necessary. But Anna couldn't take her eyes off Colin Preston.

'You didn't tell us you were bringing the family,' Mark Lewis joked as he ushered us down the stairs ahead of him. Below us, Diane Chowdry

15

took Preston's coat and disappeared for a second under the stairs.

I knew that at any moment Preston would admit he had no idea who we were, and that Anna certainly wasn't his daughter, because he had never had a daughter.

'Having a quick explore, were you?' Lewis said. 'I know what youngsters are like. Used to be one myself, you know,' he added with a hearty laugh.

But all the time his eyes were darting from Gerald Chowdry to his wife, from Diane Chowdry to Colin Preston. I got the distinct impression that Mark Lewis was a lot deeper and more intelligent than his gung-ho mateyness made him seem.

'You should have warned us,' Diane said. There was an edge to her comment. I wasn't sure what it was, but I sensed an undercurrent there. Some deeper meaning or other.

'Ye-es,' Preston said slowly. 'Sorry.' He was looking at Anna, watching her all the way down the stairs. His face betrayed no feeling at all.

'Well, you're very welcome of course,' Gerald

Chowdry said, though he didn't sound convinced. 'I'm sorry, I didn't catch your names. Didn't know you had children,' he added quietly to Preston.

'I'm Anna,' Anna said. 'Anna Preston,' she added, staring at the father who didn't know who she was. 'This is my friend, Jamie Grant,' she added, without looking at me.

'I'd better talk to Cook,' Diane Chowdry said, referring to the woman as if 'Cook' was her name rather than her job. Maybe if you have a cook that's what you do.

'We're not hungry actually,' I said. 'Be happy just to . . .' I wasn't really sure what. 'You know,' I finished a bit lamely, still surprised that Preston wasn't jumping up and down, complaining that we were nothing to do with him.

'Well, keep out of the way and be quiet,' Chowdry said. 'Find something to read. Today's papers are in the library, just along there.'

'Not upstairs, though, please,' his wife cautioned. 'Mr Prophecy is having a rest. He's rather ill, I'm afraid, and must not be disturbed.'

Chowdry turned to Lewis. 'Well, I don't know

about you, young man, but I could do with a glass of sherry.'

Anna and I were still staring at Colin Preston, who stared back at us as the Chowdrys and Mark Lewis disappeared into the drawing room.

'Dad,' Anna said quietly. Like she couldn't really believe it. Not surprisingly.

Colin Preston's blank expression resolved itself into a scowl. 'I don't know what you're playing at,' he said, his voice low and angry, 'but if I have to go along with it I will. Did *he* send you?'

Anna was shocked at his sudden change of demeanour. 'Dad?'

'And you can quit that as well,' he snapped. 'It's not at all funny.'

'Yes,' I said quickly, nudging Anna to keep quiet. '*He* sent us. I'm sorry – it's not our fault, you know. We're just as confused about all this as you are.'

'I'm not confused,' Preston hissed. 'He explained everything very clearly. It takes a bit to get your head round it, but I do understand. Oh, and I'll check it out like he said, don't you doubt that for a moment. I'm just . . .' He took a deep breath – like my dad does when he's trying not to swear in front of me and my sister, Ellie. Or rather, just Ellie. She's his only child, because of course I never existed. So far as he knows. So far as anyone knows.

'Keep out of trouble,' Preston said. 'All right? And keep out of my way.' Then he turned and hurried off to join the others in the drawing room.

'Well, I'd say that was a bit weird,' I said as casually as I could manage.

Anna turned to face me, and I was surprised and yet not surprised to see that her cheeks were wet. 'What's going on?' she said.

'I don't know,' I told her. 'But we're here to find out and that's what we're going to do.'

Her lip was going. I hate it when her lip goes. It sort of trembles, as if it's trying to say something all on its own and she's trying to stop it.

'I'm sorry,' I said. 'Oh, Anna, I'm sorry.' And I could feel my own lip trembling in sympathy with hers.

*

19

There didn't seem much point in stopping time again. Since we were here to see what would happen, we might as well let it go ahead. For now. Until something seriously weird occurred.

Not that it wasn't weird to see a ghost of Anna being dragged away by Skitters, or to have her dad, who doesn't know who she is, play along with Anna saying she's his daughter. But these were just clues – we still didn't know what the mystery was yet.

'They said we could look round, so we might as well do it,' I said. 'We'll know if something goes wrong – if time starts to go to pieces or something happens that shouldn't.'

'We hope,' Anna said. She'd recovered a bit, and apologised – though she didn't have to. 'I was just surprised, you know.'

'I know. Quite a shock.'

'There's something else,' she confessed.

'Oh? Your mum here too?' It wasn't really funny and earned me a glare.

'You asked before if I was OK. Even before we saw . . . the Skitters.'

'You just seemed on edge. You know.'

20

'I was. It's like I've been here before, though I don't really remember it. It's just sort of familiar – this house, I mean.'

'Spooky,' I said. 'Especially as you're here as a ghost.'

'It might be easier to look round once they're having their dinner,' Anna said.

'So long as we don't disturb Mr Prophecy. I wonder what's up with him. And what sort of name is that anyway?'

Anna never replied, because it was then that they told us that dinner would be another half-hour. At least, the maid came through to tell Mrs Chowdry that and we overheard.

'Wind on a bit?' I suggested when the maid had returned to the kitchen and Diane Chowdry to the drawing room. 'Get to the dinner?'

We were standing at the end of the hall away from the drawing room. There was a small library at the back of the house and Anna pulled me gently through the door. 'Wait a moment,' she said quietly. 'What's he up to?'

She knelt down so we could both peep out through the crack between the door and the

JP/2092592

frame. Mark Lewis had emerged from the drawing room.

'Back in a tick,' he called in a loud voice.

He hesitated outside the door and I realised he was making sure no one followed. Then suddenly he was in motion – hurrying to a small door under the stairs. The cupboard where the coats were hanging – where Diane Chowdry had placed Colin Preston's coat. I recognised it, a pale camel hair overcoat. Lewis pulled it towards him as he rummaged quickly – professionally – through the pockets.

'What's he doing?' I murmured.

'Up to no good,' Anna whispered back. 'Looking for something.'

Lewis was on to another coat now. He even took out a rolled umbrella, unfastened it and held it upside down to see if anything fell out. Nothing did and, with obvious disappointment, Lewis pushed it back in the cupboard and closed the door.

Then he ran quickly and quietly up the stairs.

'Come on,' Anna urged, and we hurried after him. As we went, I noticed that the cupboard

22

door had clicked back open slightly – he hadn't closed it properly.

It didn't take us long to see what he was up to. Lewis was in one of the bedrooms, going through the drawers and cupboards in a swift and efficient manner. Searching.

'Hope he doesn't disturb Mr Prophecy,' I whispered.

'I don't think he's that daft,' Anna said. 'But what's he looking for?'

'We won't know if he doesn't find it.' I led Anna back to the stairs and we tiptoed down to the hall. 'Let's give him time to finish, then we can stop time and search him. See what he's got.'

'If he takes it with him.'

'If we try to watch now, we could get caught,' I pointed out.

Anna nodded. 'We can always wind back time and see what he was up to.'

The staircase bent round in a right angle on its way down to the hall, so the two people below didn't see us. And we couldn't see them. But we froze as we recognised Colin Preston's voice.

It was urgent and low. 'I have to know,' he was saying to someone. 'And I have to know now. Before we go too far. Once we start this we can't stop – you know that.'

We didn't see the person he was talking to. But we did see Preston stride across the hall and start down the passage to the kitchen. And we heard footsteps on the marble floor as whoever he'd been speaking to returned to the drawing room – Chowdry probably.

Preston turned to look back. He seemed not to see us. He was checking the hall, not the stairs. Then he pressed on one of the large wooden panels that lined the corridor. It swung open – a door – and he stepped through. The panel swung shut behind him.

'Well, I don't know about you,' I said to Anna, 'but I think that's much more interesting than watching Mr Lewis going through the underwear drawers.'

The panel in the wall opened when you pressed it. Looking closely, I could see the hinges and a keyhole. It wasn't a secret door, then, just concealed, made to blend in.

Inside the door was a narrow stone staircase leading down. A single naked bulb lit the whitewashed walls.

'Cellars,' Anna said.

From below we heard Preston's voice echoing up to us. 'It's true,' he announced, and I could hear the awe and astonishment in his words. 'It's all true!'

Anna and I looked at each other.

'We do stop time for this,' Anna said, and I didn't disagree. I just hoped time didn't start up inconveniently again without our permission.

'What's down there?' I wondered.

'We'll soon see.'

She started quickly down the stairs and I followed close behind.

Halfway down, the whitewashed brick was replaced with sheets of metal. The cellar area at the bottom was completely encased in metal, together with a heavy door like you might find in a bank vault.

'This is weird,' I said. 'What is it? Why's it like this?'

There were several small rooms, all metal-lined.

A kitchen area with bunk beds. Like a granny flat from the future hidden down in the cellars. Tins of food were stacked in one corner, while what looked like a periscope was attached to the ceiling in another – though I could only imagine it would give a view of the room above.

'It's a shelter,' Anna said. 'Don't you have shelters?'

I shook my head. 'Do you mean it's left over from the last war?'

'No,' Anna said, and a chill ran through my whole body as I realised what she was talking about. 'I mean it's ready for the next one. This is an atomic fallout shelter.'

And then the periscope made sense. If they needed the shelter, then it was likely the house above would disappear. Completely. In a super-heated, radioactive instant.

'I'll tell you something that is weird, though,' Anna was saying.

'Oh?'

'Time is at a standstill. There's just the one door and the walls are lined with solid metal. So where did my dad go?'

I looked round, because she certainly had a point. A very worrying point.

Even more worrying was the faint, ethereal figure sitting cross-legged on the bottom bunk.

Anna. Or rather, the ghost of Anna.

Her face was streaked with tears and her hair was a mess. She looked frightened and alone.

But before either of us could wonder about that, the air was alive with Skitters. The grotesque, hideous creatures launched themselves across the room at us. Claws slashed down in a sudden frenzy of blurred movement.

Anna gave a shriek of surprise and we backed away.

Behind us, the heavy door slammed shut. And the Skitters closed in for the kill.

· CHAPTER · THREE ·

The air was a mass of claws and talons – scratching, slashing, ripping at us. Sometimes I can stop the Skitters, but my power comes and goes. I don't really know how to control it, to focus it. Or I didn't back then.

Right now it wasn't working for me and I was fighting for my life. Anna shrieked in pain as a claw raked down her face, leaving a red trail. I kicked and punched and thumped and fought. But the Skitters were driving us both back to the door. The closed door. They'd edged time on to a point where it was shut, I guessed.

But the guess brought with it a realisation.

28

'We've got to start time up again,' I yelled at Anna.

She didn't reply. She was too busy falling back against the door. A stone-like claw slammed into her and she doubled over. Leathery wings beat the air round us. A claw snagged in my hair and yanked me painfully forwards. I was desperate to reach my time dial, struggling to adjust it.

Then, abruptly, the Skitters were gone. The room was empty again, apart from me and Anna. I helped her to her feet.

'You all right?'

She nodded, breathless and pale. I traced my index finger gently along the scratch on her face and it disappeared behind my touch – the skin nudged forward in time to when it had healed.

'Thank you,' Anna said. 'What happened?'

'Time's running again,' I told her. 'I remembered, upstairs, when the Skitters vanished time started up again. They can't usually manipulate time – they exist outside it. But I thought, maybe for some reason here and now it works the other way round too. Start up time and that gets rid of them. Seems it was worth a try.'

'Seems it does. But why?'

I shrugged. 'No idea. I guess the Skitters just aren't really part of time. Not this time, as it's happening now. If we stop it, then they sort of break through.'

'From another possible sequence of events.' Anna nodded. 'That could be it, I suppose. When time is running its course they aren't a part of it. Stop time and the might-have-beens and the what-ifs are that much closer, and they find it that much easier to get in.'

'Or something. Guess we don't want to stop time again unless we really have to.'

Anna was looking round the metal room. 'Doesn't explain where Dad got to.'

Nor did it explain what the Skitters were up to – or rather, what they might have been up to or what they would be up to. And it didn't explain the ghostly image of another Anna either. Was she an Anna who was never lost like my Anna? Was she showing what might happen to the girl if she'd never been lost in time? I didn't know and I didn't ask.

Instead, I said, 'What about running time

30

backwards? Replaying events? Do you think that's safe?'

'Who knows? We could try it and see.' She turned to face me and I could tell that she was still looking flustered. 'You want to know where Dad went?'

'Don't you?'

'I don't know,' she said quietly. 'I don't know anything.'

I pretended I'd not heard. 'We wind back to the moment he arrived down here. Then we see what he does. Put ourselves a split second in the future all the time and he won't know we're here. We can see him, but he can't see us. All right?'

'Sounds like a plan,' Anna agreed.

There was no sign of ghost-Anna or the Skitters when we wound back. Not surprisingly, as they'd never really been there. A blur of movement was the clue that Colin Preston was in the room with us. I slowed time to a standstill, then immediately let it run forwards again. I didn't want to give the Skitters another chance to break through from wherever – whenever – it was they were coming from.

We sat ourselves down on the lower bunk bed, just about where ghost-Anna had been sitting. We both knew that, but neither of us mentioned it. The riveted metal door on the other side of the shelter was closed, but it soon swung heavily open and Colin Preston stepped into the room.

'Wait for the puff of blue smoke,' I whispered.

There wasn't any need to whisper, but it's kind of instinctive. You just do it. Anyway, it had the effect I was after – Anna smiled. Not much, just a slight curl of her lips. But it was enough for now.

Colin Preston – the man who was and wasn't Anna's dad – walked slowly across the shelter. He glanced back, checking he'd not been followed. Maybe he had heard Anna and me in the hall above, preparing to follow him – and find him gone.

He was muttering to himself and we strained to hear. I can play time backwards and forwards like a video or DVD, but I can't adjust the volume. So Anna and I gave up and went to stand right beside him. Not that he knew.

'Back wall,' he was muttering. 'He said the

32

back wall. He said just . . .' Preston reached out cautiously towards the wall, fingertips trembling as they approached the cold, unforgiving metal. 'He said just touch it.'

His fingers reached the metal. And passed through it, like it wasn't there. The surface shimmered and rippled as if it was made of liquid. Preston snatched his hand back and stepped away, shaking his head in disbelief.

'It's true,' he said out loud. 'It's all true!'

Then he took a deep breath and stepped through the wall. It rippled and shimmered round him, then settled back into a solid sheet of metal as he disappeared.

'A time portal,' Anna breathed. 'Hidden. Disguised as a wall. Who'd do that?'

'I think we should find out,' I said. 'And before you and I arrive down here. We were close on his heels after we heard him say that, remember?'

Anna nodded. 'Come on, then.'

She took my hand and together we stepped through the wall.

🕐 No Time

We were in a corridor. Except it wasn't like any other corridor I'd ever seen. The walls were shimmering as if in a heat haze, opaque like frosted glass. They seemed to be constantly in motion, colours swirling and blending and rippling. Like oil on a puddle, or lots of different-coloured paints not quite mixing with each other.

We'd stepped through what seemed to be a window or doorway – an opening – in the wall of the corridor. When I turned and looked back, I could see the empty shelter behind us.

As I watched, I saw myself and Anna walk in – as we had done earlier – and stare round in astonishment. It's funny looking at yourself.

'Is this where the Skitters came from?' I wondered.

'No sign of them. And they didn't come through the wall, did they?' Anna pointed out.

'So, where are we?'

'Nowhere.' Anna was walking slowly down the corridor and I could see there were other openings further along, other doors or windows or whatever they were. Portals. 'And no-when. It's a time corridor. It connects different times.'

'Right,' I said. 'Simple. I knew that.'

She stopped and turned, smiling sympathetically. 'Usually just two points in time, one at each end, are connected. This is a bit more . . .'

'Complicated?' I suggested.

'You could say that. Yes.'

I could see what she meant. There were not just two times connected by this corridor. There were dozens. Maybe hundreds – I couldn't see an end to the corridor, but I could see the openings in it stretching all the way along. I could see through some of them. And each of them opened into another time.

We paused to look through the first opening. It was like a village square, bustling and busy. At first glance it seemed to be the same time that we'd come from but somewhere in the Middle East or North Africa. I could tell it wasn't, though. I just *knew*. It was right here, the same place where the house was standing or near enough. But it was in the sixth century AD.

The next scene was mainly fields – sixteenth

century. Then a construction site, as the house itself was being built around us in 1792.

'There doesn't seem to be any order to it,' I said. 'It's just like windows on to hundreds of moments in history.'

'Just up to the mid-1950s,' Anna said as we continued along the never-ending corridor. 'There's nothing after that date. Nothing so far, anyway.'

We paused to watch people rebuilding houses after a German bombing raid in 1942; a dinosaur lumbering through heavy swampland seventy million years ago; a desolate grey wasteland where the broken remains of a tree struggled through the dust and the sky was the colour of gunmetal – earlier even than the dinosaur. Before *everything*.

Most of the scenes were dull and empty countryside, with only the abrupt changes in the weather to suggest it was a different time. Actually, even that needn't have been the case – this was England, after all.

'So where's Mr Preston?' I wondered.

'Could have wandered into any of these.'

36

'I suppose.' A thought occurred to me. 'I wonder if that's why they're arranged the way they are.'

'How do you mean?'

'I don't know, but he said "It's all true" when he found the entrance to the corridor, as if he needed to be convinced. Is that what this is? Some sort of demonstration for your dad's benefit?'

'But why? Is it to prove to him that it's possible to get through to other times?'

'It might explain why the more interesting times, the ones where it's obviously a different period, are arranged closest to where we came in. So he'll see them at once and be convinced.'

I reached out a hand and let it ripple through the opening in front of us. It was raining there – or rather, *then* – and my hand got wet. I didn't bother stepping through. I knew, I could sense, that it was possible.

'Why would anyone create this to convince my dad it's possible to travel in time?'

I didn't have an answer to that. 'We should be getting back. Time's running at normal speed while we're here. We don't want to be missed. Hey,' I said, as the thought struck me, 'will we meet ourselves coming in here?'

'I doubt it. We're here already. It only happens once, remember. We can't go back to the same moment in time. Might meet Dad, though.'

'He'll be getting back for dinner,' I said. 'Still, at least we've found the problem. A time corridor connected to a nuclear shelter. I suppose we can close it down and go home.'

'Home?' Anna raised her eyebrows.

OK, bad choice of word, especially as, if anything, this time period was her home and there was no way she could stay. Maybe that's why I didn't quibble with what she said next. Sympathy or embarrassment, take your pick.

'We can't close it down. Well, we can. I expect we could find a way. But that wouldn't really help. We need to discover why it's here and who created it. This could be a symptom rather than the cause. There's something going on that needs sorting out, but we don't know what it is yet. We might create more problems than we solve if we interfere blindly now.'

We were walking quickly back along the corridor. 'Maybe it just happened,' I suggested. 'You know, some sort of natural effect.'

'Not very likely. And what about the Skitters? What about . . . what about the images we've seen of me?'

'The you who wasn't lost,' I said. I really should think before I open my mouth sometimes.

But she didn't argue. 'If that's what it is. If that's who she is.'

'Whatever's going on,' I said gently, 'you know your dad's involved.'

'Involved maybe. But not to blame.'

'You hope.'

'I know!'

We were back at the portal into the shelter. I wondered vaguely if the ground level had changed, but it seemed more likely that the corridor could angle upwards from where it started under the house when it needed to. Not a lot of point in windows out into the middle of a bank of earth or the house's foundations. All of which reinforced Anna's belief that this wasn't natural at all, but constructed.

Planned and built. By someone, for something. But by whom, and why? What was it for?

As we stepped back into the empty fallout shelter, I decided we had altogether too many questions. It was time we started getting some answers. But that was a vain hope, because things were about to get a whole lot more bizarre.

CHAPTER FOUR

🕐 SUNDAY 11TH SEPTEMBER 1955

We had no way of knowing if Colin Preston was back in the house yet or not. But we didn't want him returning to the cellar shelter and finding us waiting for him. Whatever was happening, Anna and I reckoned it would be better to stay 'undercover' and not let on that we knew there was anything odd taking place – or that we were anything 'odd' ourselves, come to that.

So we made our way quietly back up the stairs. The door out into the passageway off the hall was closed, so I gently eased it open wide enough to peer out.

The way was clear and I was about to open the

door fully and step out when I heard footsteps in the hall.

'Hang on,' I whispered to Anna beside me. 'Someone's coming.'

She crouched down to look out from lower down, and we both saw Diane Chowdry appear from the direction of the drawing room and walk quickly towards us.

Before we could duck back into cover and close our door, Mrs Chowdry stopped. She was beside the cupboard under the stairs, looking at it curiously. Her head was tilted slightly and I guessed she'd seen that it wasn't quite closed. I remembered how it had clicked open after Mark Lewis had rummaged through the coats.

Mrs Chowdry pulled the cupboard door open fully and an umbrella clattered to the floor. It was lying half in and half out. She picked it up and reached to put it back in the cupboard. Then she hesitated and frowned. She put the umbrella away and turned her attention to the coats hanging there.

'She knows someone's been snooping,' I whispered to Anna.

'Absolutely nothing gets past you, does it?'

Just occasionally, Anna can be a bit sarcastic. Well, very sarcastic. And quite often actually.

Mrs Chowdry closed the cupboard and continued on her way. I pulled the cellar door shut and we heard her determined footsteps pass by. I waited a few moments before opening the door again.

The way was clear now, so I gestured for Anna to follow. We emerged into the hall and hurried towards the drawing room.

'What now?' Anna asked.

'Find out what Lewis is up to,' I said. 'And maybe ask your dad some searching questions. You think we can risk stopping time again?'

She shook her head. 'Not unless we have to. That ... ghost or whatever it is, it really spooks me.'

I wasn't surprised. It can't be easy seeing a faint figure of yourself abandoned in a cellar or being dragged off by nightmare creatures. I squeezed her hand and we continued across the hall.

Gerald Chowdry and Mark Lewis were in the drawing room, each holding a glass of sherry and

43

talking about the events of the previous cricket season.

'Diane has just gone to check on the status of dinner,' Chowdry told us. 'You youngsters keeping yourselves occupied?'

'Yes. Perhaps we can look at the books in your library now?' Anna asked, recalling his earlier offer.

Chowdry shrugged and turned away. 'So long as you're careful,' he mumbled, and I guessed he'd already dismissed us from his mind.

'We're always careful,' I said quietly.

Someone came into the room behind us and I thought it might be Anna's father, Preston. But it was Mrs Chowdry.

'Dinner will be in five minutes,' she announced, ignoring me and Anna. 'Where is Mr Preston?'

'He went to wash his hands,' Anna said. Probably better than telling them he'd just popped back through time in the cellar.

Mrs Chowdry continued to ignore us. 'Be a dear and go and tell him, would you, Mr Lewis?' she said.

'Of course.'

Lewis put his half-finished sherry down on a side table. As he passed Diane Chowdry, she caught his sleeve.

'Oh, and would you look in on Mr Prophecy?'

'I thought he wasn't to be disturbed,' Lewis said.

'He may wish to join us for dinner. If he's feeling better. Just knock and go in. He really won't mind.'

Lewis seemed to accept this. I guessed that he was thinking what luck it was to have permission to look in on the enigmatic Mr Prophecy and maybe search his room too.

'We'll be in the library,' I said quietly, and Anna and I slipped out of the room.

'Do we follow him?' Anna asked, meaning Lewis, who was bounding enthusiastically up the stairs.

'You do,' I told her. I'd had an idea. 'I think I'll find out a bit more about him. Where does your dad work, do you know?'

'Why?'

'Because we know he works with Chowdry, and Chowdry said Lewis was working there too.'

45

'Dad worked – when I was around, I mean – Dad worked at the War Office. But he could have changed jobs.'

'Could have,' I agreed.

'Do you think Lewis set up the time corridor in the cellar?'

'If he did, why is he searching the house? And if he knows how to manipulate time, why doesn't he stop time like we did?'

'Because of the Skitters, perhaps.'

'Perhaps. Or perhaps not. That's it, you see – we just don't know.'

Anna nodded. 'OK. I'll find out what he's up to while you find out where Dad works. Don't be long,' she added.

I grinned. 'You won't even know I've gone.'

🕐 AT THE END OF TIME

It wasn't difficult to find what I was looking for – the address of Anna's father's office. The Library at the End of Time is an enormous circular structure that has all the information you could possibly need. The only problem really is finding what you want. But I was getting quite good at that by now.

I closed the book that wasn't like any ordinary book you'd see in any ordinary library. I was about to leave when I noticed that someone was watching me. An old man was standing between two of the curving bookcases that mirrored the shape of the room as a whole. It was Senex and he was looking anxiously at me.

Senex is in charge of the Time Runners. He tells us where we're needed, and when we get back we tell him what happened and ask him about anything we don't understand. Trouble was, the last thing I'd asked him about – several times – was how is it possible for someone who's lost to get back into the real world. And his answer was simply that it isn't possible. At all. Ever.

But Anna and I had seen it happen. We'd seen a man who was lost put back as if he'd never gone, He'd been tricked into working for Darkling Midnight. He's an Adept, one of the Dark Council. A nasty piece of work is Midnight. He can do everything that Anna and I can do, and a lot more besides. But while we try to put things right and get time back on course, Midnight is forever – and I mean *forever* – trying to cause chaos and mayhem.

So, given the choice between Midnight and Senex, my instinct was to trust Senex and believe him. But from what I'd seen and experienced, my brain told me that he was lying.

'All going well?' he asked in his cracked voice.

'No problem,' I told him.

He sighed. 'I sense a barrier between us, Jamie,' he said. 'I sense you are holding back.'

'Maybe I'm not the only one.'

He nodded slowly and gestured for me to sit down again at the reading table. He sat opposite me and for a few moments said nothing. Eventually he spoke: 'The truth,' he said, 'is not always the most honest thing to tell.'

I didn't reply. If he had something to say, then he could go ahead and say it.

'You asked me if it's possible to put someone who is lost back into reality, into the normal flow of time,' Senex went on after a pause.

I nodded.

'And my answer was a lie,' Senex said.

'I know,' I replied, keeping my voice level. 'We saw it happen. Midnight can do it.'

'There are ways,' Senex admitted. 'But they are so costly. It's usually better . . .' He broke off and looked away.

'Why didn't you tell us?' I demanded. 'Why not just say yes, but there are problems?'

He looked back sharply. 'More than problems. Have you any idea what sort of upheaval . . .' He stopped and drew a deep, rasping breath. 'I am sorry – of course you don't. How could you?'

'Then tell me.' I leaned across the table, staring into his watery grey eyes. 'I want to know. I have a right to know. I'm lost – Anna and the others and I, we can never go back. Or so we thought. Are you now saying we can?'

He shook is head. 'No,' he said. 'You can't. You mustn't. Don't let Midnight or anyone else trick you into trying it. The cost would be too great, believe me.' He looked down at the surface of the table. 'Believe me,' he said again, more quietly. 'Because I know.'

I wasn't sure what he meant. I wasn't sure if I

trusted him any more now than I had before we spoke. And I am not sure how long he sat there, staring down at the table and seeing into the past – his own past. Because when he looked up, I had already gone.

🕐 Thursday 8th September 1955

They didn't have a War Office in my day. Or rather, they wouldn't have one by the time I was a boy growing up and about to be lost in time for ever. They called it the Ministry of Defence by then. Same department. Same job. Less aggressive name. A quick trip to the Library at the End of Time, where every event and person in the whole of history is recorded, and I knew where Chowdry's office was. I knew where Colin Preston's was, too. But worryingly there was no mention of Mark Lewis. Not our Mark Lewis at any rate. Which meant, I assumed, that Mark Lewis was not really the man's name at all.

I could have searched some more in the library, and I'm sure I'd have found him – whoever he was – before long. But I wanted to go and see for myself. There really is no substitute for experience.

Anna's dad, Mr Preston, was a pretty high-up civil servant, responsible for some quite sensitive stuff, it turned out. He was in charge of monitoring the research done by atomic scientists. And Chowdry was Preston's boss. He managed lots of people involved with nuclear research, including Preston – but not the non-existent Mark Lewis.

I'd chosen this day – the Thursday *before* dinner at the Chowdrys'– as that was when Chowdry had said Mark Lewis arrived, announcing that he had come to help. Whatever that meant. I stood in the corner of Chowdry's office, watching the man at work. From slightly in the future – his future – I could observe him without being seen. It was, I have to say, pretty boring. He made phone calls, he dictated memos to a secretary who looked as bored as I was feeling, he wandered about and he took a long lunch with a guy called Cecil, who was just as interesting – yawn – as Chowdry himself.

Of course, I didn't have to endure the whole day of boredom. I whizzed through it, slowing the events to normal speed every now and again to check I'd not missed anything. Even so, it was a relief when, at just before five o'clock, Mark Lewis marched into Chowdry's office and introduced himself.

'They sent me along from Logistics,' he said. 'Bit overstaffed there to be honest. Thought I could help out here. You're overdue an audit apparently. I'm to get you all ready, check the books, that sort of thing.'

'What books?' Chowdry asked warily. 'I hope you've got the necessary authorisation papers with you. We're governed by the Official Secrets Act in this office, you know.'

'Of course you are. And I've signed the Act, too. That's why they sent me along rather than that bore Hamilton. Got a chitty here authorising me to look at absolutely anything before the official bods arrive and turn the place over.' He patted his pocket. 'Signed by Sir Hilary himself.'

He seemed to be all bluster and hearty good-will, but Lewis managed to make it through the conversation and get Chowdry to agree he could inspect the books and records without ever actually producing Sir Hilary's permission slip. It was a good act, but occasionally his eyes glinted with a degree of intelligence and shrewdness that convinced me it *was* an act.

'So who are you, Mark Lewis?' I said out loud, although he'd never know it. 'Why are you really here?'

I watched him going through records and checking log books until well after dark. When everyone else had gone home, he spent an hour casually breaking into Chowdry's desk and inspecting the contents of each and every drawer. He was efficient, certainly. But why? What was he looking for?

I watched him go through Chowdry's diary. Lewis tapped a finger on the brief entry describing Sunday's upcoming dinner. I witnessed the moment he decided to invite himself along. Calculating and clever.

Well, I could be clever too, and I wound time back.

Lewis walked backwards out of the office, then raised his hand to knock. I followed him as he walked – backwards – through the War Office and out into the street. I slowed the backwards motion of time so I could follow the taxi that drove (backwards) towards Lewis's point of departure. It was a nondescript office block at Cambridge Circus.

I sped Lewis back through a meeting with a grey-haired man in a tweed suit who smoked a pipe and waited until he was sitting at what I assumed was his desk. There was nothing to give away his real name, no personal belongings. Not even a family photo.

Then I let events unfold in the proper direction and at the right speed. Lewis took a phone call – from his boss, judging by how polite and deferential he was. Of course, he'd be there right away.

I followed him into the office to meet the pipe-smoking man in the tweed suit. I watched as the man greeted him and handed him a folder of papers.

'Thank you for coming so promptly, George,' the tweed man said.

'You did say it was urgent, sir.'

'Yes,' the man agreed. 'I have a little job for you. At the War Office. Following that anonymous tip-off last week, we've traced things to Chowdry's mob, but we can't be any more specific than that at the moment, I'm afraid. Still, that is where the call came from, so it seems that someone there knows something and wants to help.'

'Why aren't they being more obvious and open about it, then?'

'Hard to say. Perhaps they're scared. Perhaps they don't really know any more than they've already told us. But whatever the reason, I want you to go in, poke about and see what you can find. Maybe identify our source, or even the traitor himself.'

Lewis – or rather 'George' – was leafing through the documents and papers in the file he had just been given. 'So, I'm Mark Lewis from Logistics,' he said.

'Can't afford for you to use your own name. Someone there may have heard of George Rorke.' He put his pipe to one side and clasped his hands together on the desk in front of him.

'This is a serious business, George. I have a choice – either to send in an agent to find out what's going on or to mobilise a security team to do things rather more forcefully. You're the best man I've got, and we need results, not bodies. Let me give you some background.'

Five minutes later and I knew exactly what Mark Lewis – real name George Rorke – was up to and why.

True to my word, I was only gone from Chowdry's house for a minute at most.

But it was enough. When I got back there, everything had changed and everything I had just learned was no longer even true.

⏱ SUNDAY 11TH SEPTEMBER 1955

Anna was on the landing at the top of the stairs.

'Got him,' I said to her as soon as I arrived. 'I know all about the mysterious Mark Lewis and what he's up to.'

'That's great,' Anna said, though she didn't sound as enthusiastic or excited as I'd hoped.

'Knew you'd be impressed,' I told her.

Anna looked at me, puzzled. 'So, where have you been?' she asked. 'And who's Mark Lewis?'

I have to admit, that surprised me. I probably gaped like a goldfish. Then I laughed. But Anna was being totally serious. She really didn't know who or what I was talking about.

'Where do you think I just went?' I asked her when it was obvious she wasn't kidding around.

'Well, I don't know, do I? I was with you just now. I didn't know you'd been anywhere else.'

'There was a man,' I said, trying to keep my expression as serious as possible so she wouldn't think I was joking or teasing. 'Mark Lewis, or at least that's what he said his name was.'

'It sounds familiar,' she confessed. 'I'm sure I know that name. But then it's one of those ordinary sorts of names, isn't it?'

'Please – think!' I urged. 'Try to remember. What's happened to Mark Lewis?'

'But I don't know who he is.' She sat down on the landing, cross-legged. 'Something's happened, hasn't it? Something to do with time. Something's changed.'

I knelt beside her. 'Yes, something's changed. This man, Lewis, was here. A guest for dinner. Chowdry said he just turned up to work in his office last week and then invited himself along this evening.'

'But if he was here, how come I don't remember?'

'I went to find out about him, to see where he really came from and what he was up to. He was searching the rooms and going through the coats.'

'Mrs Chowdry opened the cupboard,' Anna said slowly as she remembered. 'The door wasn't closed and an umbrella fell out.'

'That's right. The umbrella that Lewis

examined. He didn't put it back properly and he didn't quite close the door.'

'I . . .' She rubbed her eyes. 'Yes,' she said at last. 'I can almost remember. It's like when you have something on the tip of your tongue – a name or a face you can't quite bring to mind. It's almost there. I can sort of feel that what you're saying happened. Only . . .' She looked up at me. 'Only time has changed somehow, and it didn't.'

'No,' I agreed. 'It didn't. Things have changed, just in the moments I've been gone. I don't know why – maybe it was something Lewis did. But whatever the reason, time has switched on to a different track – a time line in which Lewis is no longer here. He was never here. He never came to this house at all.'

'So where is he?'

'I don't know.' I thought about that. 'I guess his boss never sent him for some reason.'

'Sent him where? Who is he anyway?'

'And why did someone want him out of the way?'

Lots of good questions there. Fortunately I had

the answers – or I thought I did. Some of them anyway.

'Come on,' I said. 'I'll show you.'

How wrong I was.

🕐 Thursday 8th September 1955 (again)

I didn't show Anna. I couldn't. We arrived in the same office, just a bit earlier, so I could show her where Lewis – or rather Rorke, as that was his real name – worked.

'MI5,' I said. 'Or whatever it's called these days. Security service anyway.'

I led her through a frozen office. Men and a few women were caught at their desks – on the telephone, writing notes, typing at an old-fashioned typewriter. Well, that's not really fair. It was probably a very modern typewriter, given this was 1955, but you know what I mean. It was all pretty much exactly as I remembered.

Until we got to the desk where I'd found Lewis before (or later, actually, as I'd not arrived yet). He wasn't there. Not only wasn't he there, but a middle-aged woman with grey curly hair was closely examining grainy photographs of men in raincoats.

'So,' Anna said slowly, 'he dresses as a woman and wears a wig when he's at the office, does he?'

It's difficult sometimes to know if she's joking. But I think she was.

'I must have got the wrong desk,' I said, looking round. But I hadn't.

We wound on, and the woman took a phone call – just as Lewis had a few minutes later . . . She went through to the office where Lewis had met the tweedy man with his pipe, and Anna and I followed.

'I want you to get Blackler and his team ready to go,' the pipe-smoker told the grey-haired woman. 'This weekend probably, but I'll issue the M-19 form as soon as I can get clearance.'

'Very good, sir,' the woman said. 'I suppose,' she added hesitantly, 'that this is the best option.'

The man shook his head. 'Only option. If I had someone I could spare to work on the inside and get us more data, I'd do it. There's an audit due soon, so we could get them in under cover of that, say they're from Logistics, come to tidy up or whatever. We might even find out who sourced the information in the first place. But you know as well as I do, there's no one.'

'What about ...' The woman broke off and frowned. 'You know ...' She gave a short laugh and shook her head. 'I'm sorry, sir. For a moment, I thought. No – you're right, of course. There's no one free who could do it. I'll alert Blackler and his team.'

'Thank you.' The man started to fill his pipe from a leather pouch of tobacco. The woman returned to her desk and took out a grey-covered phone book.

Anna and I faded away. As if we'd never been there.

🕐 SUNDAY 11TH SEPTEMBER 1955

Mark Lewis didn't exist. Not anywhere.

'He's lost, isn't he?' I said as soon as we were back on the landing in Chowdry's house. 'Mark Lewis – or George Rorke – he's been ...' Well, he hadn't been killed exactly. It was worse than that.

'If that's true,' Anna said, 'and I'm not doubting it,' she added quickly, 'that means something here is really wrong.'

'Wrong and dangerous. Time corridor, your dad, secret agents going missing, your ghost and a horde of Skitters. Not good,' I summarised.

'Not good at all,' Anna agreed. She closed her eyes for a few moments. 'I'm trying to remember,' she said after a while. 'Trying to think back.'

We couldn't just roll back time and see what had happened to Lewis. It doesn't work like that. The past had changed. It would look very different and he wouldn't be there. We couldn't do it any more than you can drive back through a town that's just been hit by a mega earthquake and expect it to look the same as it did yesterday. Or record something on a video, then wind back and expect to see what was on the tape before you recorded over it.

'I followed him upstairs.' I could hear the strain in Anna's voice as she struggled to recall events. It hadn't really happened – things had changed – but she could see through the differences, she could remember the way events had been before someone or something changed them. But it sounded as if it was immense effort. 'We came up from the cellar, from the shelter. You went to check on . . . to check on Lewis,' she realised. She opened her eyes, smiling triumphantly as she did remember, as she broke through the fences and walls that time can put up round us when we're not looking. It's not really like losing your memory – for Anna it really never happened. Time changed things and she never saw Lewis. But like me, being outside time, she can get round its little tricks. Sometimes.

'That's right,' I said. 'I went to check on Lewis and you followed him upstairs. Up here. That's why you were on the landing.'

Anna knew it now. It was as if she'd broken through the barrier that prevented her remembering what had happened. It was clearer for her now. 'I was watching him. I saw him go through to that room.' She pointed along the corridor.

'Mrs Chowdry asked him to check on Mr Prophecy,' I remembered.

Anna nodded. 'And that's what he did. He opened the door, went in . . .'

'And then?'

'The door closed behind him.' She was staring down the corridor as she remembered. 'Then – nothing. He was gone.' She looked back at me. Nervous, anxious, fearful. 'Something happened to him in that room.'

I was feeling just as anxious. 'And there's only one way to find out what it was,' I said.

We stood outside the door, neither of us wanting to open it, both of us knowing that we must.

'If you're already lost,' I whispered, 'can you be, like, lost again?'

'How would I know?'

'Just wondered.'

'Maybe we're about to find out.'

'Yeah,' I said. 'Maybe.'

And I opened the door.

It was just a room. A bedroom. A very ordinary bedroom. With a bed in it. OK, there was a dressing table, and a wardrobe too. There was a connecting door in the side wall that led into the next room.

We stood inside, pulling the door gently closed.

'Now what?' I whispered. I was whispering because I was nervous and also because there was someone in the bed.

We couldn't see who it was, though I guessed it was the frail and infirm Mr Prophecy. The covers were humped over him and pulled up above his head. He was absolutely still. Instinctively, we both crept closer, wanting to see the enigmatic gentleman. Was it Mr Prophecy who had somehow sent Lewis into non-existence? Was he the one who was playing around with the flow of time?

'You do realise,' I whispered even more quietly as we edged closer, 'that this is the room we saw the Skitters drag *you* into.'

'That wasn't me,' Anna hissed back. 'Anyway, I'm not in here now, am I?'

I knew what she meant, so I didn't disagree. But at that precise moment it wasn't Anna's ghost

I was worried about meeting. I could feel a tightness in my stomach – a warning that something was about to go horribly wrong. My view of Mr Prophecy – of the bed right in front of me – was blurred and indistinct. As if there was something else in the way.

Something alive. Something moving, just on the edge of my consciousness.

Anna and I both realised what it was at the same moment.

'The Skitters,' she said. 'They're still in here!'

I didn't have time to agree. I didn't need to. The air erupted around us as the blurred, misty shimmers took on solid shape and form. Three stone-faced imp-like creatures launched themselves at us from in front of the bed. Leathery wings beat the air and claws slashed towards us.

I pushed Anna quickly behind me as we backed away. But one of the Skitters had got round the other side of us and was blocking the way back to the door. I might be able to stop them, to hold them off, if there were only three. But as we watched, several more of the creatures shimmered into existence on the bed, leaping up and charging towards us.

One of the Skitters lashed out at me and I caught its hand – if you can call it a hand – in mine. Its claws convulsed, then seemed to flake away, withering as time took its toll. In a second the thing was a pile of grey dust scattered across the carpet.

But there were too many for me to stop them all. And it only needed one of them to get to Anna.

With the way we'd come in now blocked, Anna had backed over to the connecting door. She turned quickly to open it while I prepared to fight off more of the Skitters. They were slightly wary now that I'd managed to destroy one of them. But that wouldn't last.

'It's locked!' Anna yelled as she desperately tried to open the door.

'Let me.' I risked turning away, and heard the cries of triumph as the Skitters came at us. I was relying on instinct. Hoping that somehow I'd do it.

The handle turned, the door opened – moved

back in time to a moment when it was unlocked. Anna and I tumbled through, and Anna slammed the door behind us. Like that would do any good. If they wanted, the Skitters could smash it down, or age it to dust, just as I'd done to one of them.

But nothing happened. We held our breath – Anna standing scared but defiant in front of the door, me sprawled rather inelegantly on the floor. And still nothing happened.

'Perhaps they can't leave the room,' I said as I got up. 'Perhaps they're guarding whatever's in there.'

'Mr Prophecy,' Anna said. 'Whoever he might be.'

'And who might *you* be?' a voice demanded from behind us.

I hadn't thought there would be someone in the room. It was a bedroom like the one we'd just left – a mirror image.

Except that the bed was covered with large sheets of paper – plans, schematics, blueprints and drawings. Sitting in among them, interrupted from her task of examining the papers, a pencil in one hand, was a woman. She was thirty-two years old, fair-haired and wearing rather severe horn-rimmed spectacles.

In the hand that wasn't clutching the pencil, she was holding a gun. And she was pointing it at me and Anna.

CHAPTER SIX

Nobody moved. Not because time was standing still or anything. We just looked at each other. Or rather, the woman looked at us, and Anna and I looked at the gun.

After a few moments, the woman decided we weren't worth the effort and tossed the pistol on the bed beside her.

'What are you doing in my room?' she asked.

'Sorry,' I said.

'We were . . .' Anna started. She glanced at me. I guess she realised she couldn't really tell this woman that we'd been escaping from killer imp-like demons from outside time.

'We were checking on Mr Prophecy,' I said. 'In

72

the next room. Didn't realise there was anyone in here. Sorry.'

'Sorry,' Anna echoed.

The woman was frowning. 'And just who are you? There's only supposed to be Mr and Mrs Chowdry here this evening, and Mr Preston. Until . . .' Her voice faded, and neither of us answered. She looked pointedly at the gun.

'I'm Jamie,' I told her. 'This is Anna. She's my friend.'

'And why are you here?' the woman asked.

'I'm Mr Preston's daughter,' Anna said levelly.

The woman's eyes narrowed. Then she laughed. 'You're not a very good liar,' she said. 'I happen to know that Mr Preston doesn't have a daughter.'

'No,' Anna said, so quietly that I only just caught her words. 'No, he doesn't.'

'How do you know Mr Preston?' I asked.

She gave me a grown-up look – one that was somewhere between contempt and irritation. 'We work together,' she said. 'All right?' She took a deep breath. 'Look, my name is Barbara Aitken. And I'm not really going to shoot you.

73

But I do need to know who you are and why you are here. Tonight of all nights.'

'What's special about tonight?' Anna asked.

'Never you mind.'

I was looking at the plans and drawings spread across the bed. I thought about just stopping time so I could study them properly. But if I did that, the Skitters might be back with a vengeance. I couldn't risk that. Maybe it would be enough just to ask the question. 'So what sort of work do you do?'

'I can't tell you.'

'Don't you know?' Anna said.

'*I* know, yes. But you shouldn't. It's . . . secret.'

'I see.'

I was still looking at the sheets of paper. Barbara Aitken turned several of them over. But I'd seen enough to know they were plans, blueprints and definitions for building something. I had no idea what. But I reckoned I could find out.

I reached out carefully and brushed my fingers over the sheets on the bed.

'Leave those alone,' Barbara Aitken warned. Her hand was moving towards the gun again.

But I barely heard her, barely saw what she was doing. I was miles – or rather, years – away.

⏰ THURSDAY 8TH MAY 1958

She was the only woman in among a group of men. I recognised Barbara Aitken by her glasses as much as anything. She was wearing a rather severe grey suit and standing with several severe men. They were grey too – grey suits, grey faces, grey expressions.

We were in a huge building. I thought at first it was a warehouse, but then I saw the large aeroplanes arranged at the other end, the enormous sliding double doors, and I realised that we were in an aircraft hangar. Well, I wasn't really there, not so anyone else could tell.

'I can't understand how the Soviets got wind of what we were up to,' one of the grey men was saying as I walked over to join the group.

They were standing close to one of the huge, dark planes. The RAF roundel was the only splash of colour on its body. The propellers were as big as I was and the whole thing towered over us. But all the attention was focused on the belly of the plane.

Barbara Aitken looked away as another man said, 'We should have been years ahead of them. But from what MI6 says, their designs are pretty well identical to our own. How could that happen?' he asked pointedly, looking round.

'Doesn't matter,' another man said. 'The main thing is that it's finished. And once we get it down to Australia we'll find out if it works.'

'It will work,' the first man said. 'The Russian one worked when they tested it last month. And, let's face it, whether we admit it or not, their design is identical to ours.'

As they spoke, I edged round them to see what they were looking at. And when I saw it, everything else fled from my mind. All I could see was the dark cylinder, almost two metres long, nestling on a trolley beneath the open underbelly of the aircraft.

'You're working on a bomb,' I said as the room swam back into focus around me. 'Aren't you? That's what these blueprints and plans are for – it's a bomb. An atom bomb.'

'How could you know that?' she snapped in shocked surprise.

'You'd never believe me.'

She had grabbed the gun again, though she looked more nervous now than threatening. As if we'd found out her guilty secret.

But that wasn't it, I realised. Replaying the snatches of conversation from the hangar, I reckoned there was an even more guilty secret lurking here.

'Why do you have all these plans here with you?' I asked.

'Yes,' Anna agreed. 'Why bring them here? Shouldn't they be locked away in a safe or something?'

'It's none of your business,' she said abruptly. But I caught an edge of nervousness – of fear even.

'You're a spy!' I told her. 'That's what's going on here, isn't it? You smuggled these plans out of the laboratory or wherever you work. You're going to give them to the Russians, the Soviets – somehow.' That was how the Russian bomb was going to be exactly the same as the British one I'd seen.

'Don't be ridiculous.' Her forehead was sheened with perspiration.

Anna was staring at the woman in angry disbelief. I guess that as she grew up in this time period, it meant a lot to her. She had a real idea of just how close the world was to annihilation. Britain, America and Russia in a nuclear stand-off, with atom bombs ready to go at the first attack of nerves or international misunderstanding.

'You traitor!' Anna accused. 'People like you will destroy the world.'

Barbara Aitken was shaking, the gun wavering so much she wouldn't have been able to shoot us if she tried. Her eyes were welling up with tears. 'I'm trying to *save* the world – can't you see?'

Anna laughed. 'Oh, and how do you do that by giving away your country's secrets?'

'Don't you understand? That's the only way. As soon as one side in this Cold War has a great enough advantage it will start – they'll destroy the other. Just to be sure they don't get blown up first.'

'That's mad,' I said.

She gave a nervous laugh. 'How right you are. In every sense. That's what we call it – MAD. Mutually Assured Destruction. So long as each side knows that if they attack, the other side will retaliate and wipe them out, no one will start a war. But if one side gets an overwhelming advantage, they'll press it home fast – before the other side can catch up. Fuchs had the right idea,' she went on, quieter and less emotional now. 'Klaus Fuchs gave the Russians our atomic secrets until he was caught in 1950. Someone has to carry that on.'

'But it won't work,' Anna said. 'It'll just give the Soviets the advantage and then *they'll* attack first.'

Barbara Aitken shook her head. 'No. They

promised. If I give them our latest development plans, they will give us their secrets in return. Don't you see? There are people on both sides working for peace, for a level playing field so that neither side will ever fire the first shot.'

I was wishing I knew more about the Cold War right now. I did know that the world hadn't ended in atomic war back in the 1950s. The Soviet Union and America were in a stand-off – each with nuclear weapons aimed at the other and ready to fire. But it never happened. Despite the arguments and the flash points, the rhetoric and the posturing, neither side ever had the need to fire on the other. Or the guts or the insanity or the whatever it took to end the world.

But the question was – did we all survive because of Barbara Aitken or was this some corruption of history that would lead to the nuclear holocaust she was so desperate to prevent.

'You work for my ... for Preston?' Anna asked.

The woman didn't answer, but we could see from her expression that this was true.

Anna looked at me. 'Then I think we should tell him what's going on,' she whispered.

'He may already know,' I said quietly. 'Remember, Lewis was looking for evidence of a spy in Chowdry's organisation. MI5 or whoever they are already know.'

'And someone erased him,' Anna said. 'Removed him from history.' She was looking directly at Barbara Aitken.

Could she have done it? This slightly dowdy-looking lady with her horn-rimmed glasses who was looking at us, confused and nervous – could she have condemned a man to never existing? Maybe she could, I decided – if she thought it was a choice between that and the end of the world.

'It was in someone's interests. Someone with the ability to manipulate time. To get rid of Lewis – wipe him out. Whatever happened,' I said, 'the security services were investigating, and probably still are. So Preston may already know.' I turned to Barbara Aitken, who had obviously been listening to us. She was probably wondering what two children knew about it all. 'Does Preston know?' I demanded. 'Because if he doesn't, then we have to tell him. If he does, then perhaps – just perhaps – we don't have to take this any further.' I wasn't sure what I meant by that. I was just trying to unsettle her a little bit more – enough to tell us what was going on here.

'Of course he knows,' Barbara Aitken snapped, impatient rather than frightened now. 'I don't have to justify myself to two youngsters like you,' she said sternly.

'You don't have to tell us anything,' I agreed. 'But if you don't we'll go and ask Mr Preston. And Mr Chowdry. And anyone else we can find who might know – or be interested. There's a man called Lewis at the War Office . . .'

'You're not frightening me,' she said. But I could see in her eyes that I was. 'Because it's all official,' she insisted. 'Or nearly. I couldn't do this without some help. I couldn't set up a meeting with the top Soviet spy in Britain on my own.'

'What are you saying?' Anna's face was red, maybe with anger or maybe with embarrassment.

'Colin Preston is my superior. He's as aware as

I am of how the world works, and what will happen if the balance of power shifts too much one way or the other. He set this up.'

Anna was staring at her open-mouthed. I took Anna's hand, but she shook it free and stepped away from Barbara Aitken, away from me.

'And he was in the time corridor,' Anna said. 'It was him. He got rid of Lewis too, before Lewis could uncover the truth.'

'Anna,' I said quietly. 'We can't be sure . . .'

But she cut me off. 'Oh yes, we can.' She turned towards me, and a tear escaped from her eye and ran down her cheek. 'My father's a spy. A traitor. And a murderer.'

'We don't know that,' I said.

'Don't we?'

Barbara Aitken was looking at us as if we were mad. 'Murder? What are you children talking about?'

I suppose it was good that the mention of murder had distracted her from the fact that she had just heard her childless boss described as Anna's father. But not very.

'We have to go,' I said.

I took Anna by the arm and led her out into the corridor, leaving Barbara Aitken staring after us. She looked as if she was going to follow, but then changed her mind. Perhaps she wasn't supposed to be here, but she must have been worried about what we might tell people. Or did they all know already? Certainly, Anna's dad was involved, and it seemed a good bet that Chowdry was in on it too. This was his house and his dinner party after all.

'What about the Skitters?' I said to Anna as soon as we were alone in the corridor. I pointed to the door to Mr Prophecy's room. 'In there and dragging away the ghost-image of you.'

'What about them?' she asked sulkily. OK, she wasn't really sulking – she was anxious and upset and worried. She does sulk sometimes. But this was different.

'Well, I don't think your dad has anything to do with them, that's what.'

'How do you know?'

'I don't know, not for sure. But down in the cellar – you remember – the time corridor thing. He was surprised it was there.'

Anna seemed to brighten. 'That's right. And he said something about it being true, as if someone had sent him there to see it for himself, to convince him.'

'That's right. So I don't think he wiped out Lewis.' I took a deep breath, not sure how she'd react to what I was going to say next. Not sure that I should even say it. But Anna would be thinking it anyway, and I didn't want her to get the idea I was daft, or not telling her everything that was on my mind. 'Your father may be a spy,' I said quietly, 'but he isn't a murderer.'

She took it quite well actually. Anna's not daft either. 'Then he's being manipulated,' she said. 'Someone has been mucking around with time and they've somehow convinced Dad he's doing the right thing.'

'Mucking around with time,' I repeated. 'Is that a technical term?'

She didn't rise to it. She was thinking too hard to even realise I was joking. Mucking about. 'Skitters, time corridors . . .' she murmured.

'Could be this mysterious Mr Prophecy we haven't met properly yet.'

'Or it could be someone we have met. Several times.' Anna was biting her lower lip like she does when she's nervous and worried. 'Think about it. Skitters, lost people, the fact we can't safely stop time.'

'And atomic secrets.' I had to admit this wasn't sounding so good. 'Someone who wants to heat up the Cold War.'

'Midnight,' Anna said quietly.

It seemed likely – probable even. Darkling Midnight is a Runner. Only he's not like us, he's on the other side. The *dark* side. He's not interested in making sure time runs smoothly and everything goes as history wants. Quite the opposite. He's only interested in wrecking things – in tearing down the established order and wiping out, well, everything.

He says that he and his people want to erase it all so they can build something better in its place. But is that right? And who are they to decide what's better or worse? I just know that to get to where they want to be, they have to destroy everything. And that can't be right.

'Midnight,' I agreed.

From the hallway below we heard the sound of the doorbell.

'That'll be him now,' I joked. Only of course it

wasn't much of a joke. And we hurried to see who it really was, dreading that I might be right.

Anna was all for running down the stairs, but I held her back. We watched through the banisters, as we had earlier when Colin Preston – Anna's dad – arrived. If it was Midnight, I wanted to be as far away from him as possible and out of sight.

Diane Chowdry was in almost as much of a hurry as Anna. Her heels clicked rapidly on the floor below as she went to answer the door.

Her husband was less impressed. 'It's Sunday evening,' he complained loudly from the drawing-room door. 'Just about to have dinner, for goodness' sake. Who on earth can it be?'

But his wife knew. She all but tore open the front door and immediately embraced the large man standing there. He was just a silhouette against the night outside.

'Mikhail,' Mrs Chowdry said, 'you're here at last.'

'My dear Diane,' a deep, heavily accented voice replied.

Anna and I looked at each other. It didn't sound like Midnight. Mikhail didn't sound his style either – I mean, Mik Midnight? Do me a favour.

Below us, the man stepped into the hallway. And sure enough – happily enough – it was not Midnight. He was a large man, broad and dark-haired with a closely trimmed black beard. He was carefully removing his leather gloves, easing them off finger by finger.

Behind him was a small man with pinched features. He was completely bald, and wearing a pale raincoat with his hands thrust deep into the pockets, he looked even more sinister than Mikhail.

Chowdry joined his wife. 'Who is this?' he demanded. 'You know these people, dear?' He gave an audible gasp as he inspected the tall man more closely. 'But surely – aren't you . . .' His voice faded and even from the stairs we could see his fear.

'Mikhail Rasnitov,' the man said. 'Cultural Attaché at the Soviet Embassy. At your service.' He smiled, and there was nothing at all cultured about it. 'Or rather, at your wife's service, just as she has been at mine for so many years now.'

Chowdry was looking from his wife to the Russians and back again. You could see his expression changing as he worked it out.

His wife wasn't wasting time waiting for him to get there, though. 'I'm afraid we're a couple of places short for dinner now,' she said.

'Krasny will not be joining us,' Mikhail Rasnitov said. The bald man – Krasny – inclined his head slightly in agreement. 'And neither,' Rasnitov went on, 'will your husband.'

Chowdry did understand that. 'Now, see here!' he protested.

But Krasny stepped forward, pulling his right hand out of his coat pocket. He was holding a small pistol.

Chowdry backed away. He looked at his wife. 'What *is* going on?'

'Oh, haven't you understood anything?' She sighed theatrically. 'I'm a spy, darling. Got it now? All those fascinating little chats we've had. All that technical jargon you told me not to worry my silly head about as I wouldn't understand it. All of that, well, I passed it on to Mikhail. He was kind enough to explain things properly. You have no idea how far a little attention and interest will go.'

Chowdry was white-faced. 'And how far have *you* gone?'

'Far enough. There's no going back now.' She turned away from him. 'I'd put him in the cellar. It's quite secure down there.'

Krasny gestured with the gun and Chowdry walked slowly back across the hall towards the cellar. He seemed older now, shuffling along with his head bowed – though whether in shame, embarrassment or sadness it was impossible to tell. Anna and I drew back into the shadows as they passed below us.

'Is the good Dr Aitken here?' Rasnitov asked. He and Diane Chowdry were walking arm in arm towards the drawing room. I could see that in his free hand Rasnitov was holding a briefcase.

'And Mr Preston.' She paused while her husband unleashed a stream of abuse from further down the hall. Then the cellar door slammed shut and his voice was cut off. 'We thought we'd talk over dinner.'

'And our other . . . friend?'

'Mr Prophecy is upstairs.' She laughed. 'He won't be joining us for dinner.'

Rasnitov was laughing too as they disappeared into the drawing room.

'Let's hope she's forgotten we're here,' I said. 'I don't fancy being locked down in the shelter with Mr Chowdry.'

'We know how to get out,' Anna said.

'Good point,' I conceded.

'Anyway, it's the 1950s. Children keep out of the way. She probably doesn't care. Doesn't think we're worth bothering about in the slightest. We're just kids.'

'And your dad?'

Anna shrugged. 'I don't know. I really don't know.'

We were sitting at the top of the stairs. 'I still don't see what this has to do with us,' I said. 'I mean, apart from your dad being here, and that could be a coincidence. There's spying, Cold War intrigue and stuff. But what's with the time corridor and the Skitters and everything? What have they got to do with it all?'

'Unless you want to risk playing about with time and getting skittered, we'll have to wait and see.'

'I don't want to wait and see,' I protested. I took something from my pocket – a small transparent sphere about the size of a golf ball. It was something I'd collected on a previous mission – to future America – with Anna. 'I wonder if this could help somehow. Maybe allow us to stop time without bringing the Skitters back to get us.'

She recognised it at once. 'The time synchronisation coordinator you took from Kustler's experiments.'

'That's right.'

'But I don't see how you can use that to stop time any more than we can right now.'

'It somehow allows us in and out of time, remember. Midnight implied it was how he managed to replace someone who was lost, how he put them back into history.'

'With vast amounts of energy,' Anna pointed

out. 'Which we don't have. And even if we did, we don't know how – or *if* – that thing works.'

'No,' I admitted. I'd been clutching at straws as I drowned in a lack of ideas. 'Neither do I. But there must be something we can do.'

'Yes. Like I said – we wait.'

'And like I said, I don't want to. And actually, I don't think we have to,' I went on. I hadn't really thought it through, but an idea was forming in my mind. A theory. I stuffed the little sphere back into my pocket. 'Think about the Skitters. We've come across them up here on the first floor but nowhere else. There must be a reason. They were close to or inside the room where Lewis was lost and your ghost was dragged away.'

'And they were in the cellar, in the shelter.'

'But that's where the time corridor is hidden. Whatever it's for. And your ghost appeared down there, too.'

'So?'

'So maybe the Skitters are just keeping close to those time disruptions. They didn't follow us into Barbara Aitken's room.'

'Dr Aitken,' Anna corrected me – we knew

94

that now from what Rasnitov had said to Diane Chowdry. But I'd got her thinking. 'Maybe,' she decided at last. 'Maybe you're on to something there.'

'Worth risking?'

She bit her lip and nodded. 'Worth risking,' she agreed.

So we risked it.

'So far, so good,' I said as events speeded up.

We watched Colin Preston come upstairs at ninety miles an hour – or so it seemed to us – and he and Dr Aitken went back down. She was carrying the papers and plans from the bed rolled up and under her arm. I wondered what, if anything, she'd told Preston or anyone else about our visit. With luck, she too would have dismissed us as nosy youngsters and not worry any more about it.

More confident now that the Skitters were not about to burst through the thin walls of time and attack us, we joined the dinner party. The maid from the kitchen served, glancing nervously round at the guests – wondering no doubt who they were and where Mr Chowdry had gone. Perhaps Mrs Chowdry had invented some vague excuse. Or maybe she just didn't care what the servants thought – that's communist equality for you.

Preston and Dr Aitken sat nervously next to each other, neither of them eating much. Mrs Chowdry and the Russian, Rasnitov, made up for it with their very healthy appetites. Krasny sat apart, close to the door, so he could see across the hall. His attention rarely left the concealed cellar door in the passage to the kitchen.

We fast-forwarded through the meal, slowing things down as the coffee arrived and Rasnitov dabbed at his beard with a linen napkin.

'Now, to business,' he declared. 'You have the plans?'

He knew she had, and Barbara Aitken produced the roll of papers from under her chair.

'Excellent.' Rasnitov cleared a space on the table. He did this by sweeping aside the cutlery and crockery, glasses and candlesticks. The candles were alight, but that probably wasn't the only reason why Diane Chowdry let out a cry of surprise and dismay as her best crockery shattered on the polished wooden floor.

'That was good!' I exclaimed.

Anna and I were a micro-second ahead of things, so they couldn't hear us. As if we weren't there, which really we weren't.

Anna grinned. She was impressed too.

So I rolled it back a bit and let Rasnitov sweep the table clear again. And again. And once more for luck.

We were both laughing, Anna and I. She imitated Diane Chowdry's shriek, and we paused things till we'd recovered.

'Sorry,' I said. 'But it was getting a bit serious.'

'Still is,' Anna said. She was still smiling, though. 'And still no Skitters,' she pointed out. Which was good.

We let Rasnitov get on with it, and he unrolled the plans and papers across the table. Krasny joined him and together they examined them, nodding and looking smug.

'They have to be back first thing tomorrow,' Dr Aitken said nervously.

'Oh, I doubt that. I suspect your office will

have other things on their mind,' Rasnitov said, though he didn't explain what he meant. 'But Krasny can photograph them, don't worry.'

Dr Aitken looked relieved. Preston was frowning. Mrs Chowdry was trying to fit the pieces of a plate together. I reckoned it was more than just the crockery in her life that was broken beyond repair.

'You brought the plans for us?' Preston asked. He didn't look or sound quite as nervous as his colleague, but he was rattled nonetheless.

Rasnitov paused long enough to hand over his briefcase. Preston found himself a spare bit of table and opened it. Inside were sheaves of papers and he lifted them out excitedly.

'Barbara, come and look at these.'

'No need to return them,' Rasnitov said without looking up. 'They are yours to keep.'

Dr Aitken was already leafing through them. 'Not as advanced as we thought, even,' she said quietly to Preston.

'Hang on,' I said. And time stopped.

'What is it?' Anna asked.

We walked round the room, glancing at

Rasnitov and Krasny, stepping over Diane Chowdry, arriving beside Dr Aitken and Preston.

'If I understand it properly,' I said, 'they're swapping secrets. Atomic secrets, yes?'

'That's right. You show me yours and I'll show you mine. To maintain the balance of power.'

'And Dr Barbara has smuggled out the latest atomic bomb details and research to show Rasnitov.' I reached across and pressed my hand down flat on the nearest of her papers. 'This was printed just last week.' I touched another and felt its age too. 'This one eleven days ago.'

'As you'd expect.'

'They're being sold out,' I said. I reached past Barbara Aitken and rubbed the paper she was holding gently between my thumb and forefinger.

'How do you mean?'

'This isn't the latest Soviet research. It's years out of date. This was printed in 1949.' I brushed my fingers along another sheet. 'This blueprint is over fourteen months old.'

'Maybe they've made slow progress since,' Anna said. But she sounded dubious.

'The most important research project they

have going and nothing's been invented or discovered for over a year? Right.'

'Right,' Anna said. 'Or rather, wrong.'

'Very wrong.'

'So what happens next?' Anna wondered.

'Let's see.'

'Excellent,' Rasnitov announced as time started up again. 'Though I confess this is merely a distraction. You have it upstairs, you say?'

He was speaking to Diane Chowdry. When she didn't answer, he pulled her to her feet. 'Upstairs?' he repeated.

'What? Oh yes. Upstairs.'

We followed the little procession that headed for Mr Prophecy's room. I think, looking back, that they all knew except Barbara Aitken. She seemed confused and wary.

Right up until they went into the room. Mrs Chowdry led the way. She didn't knock, just opened the door and stood aside to let the others in. Anna and I followed.

'Watch out for Skitters,' I said.

But there were none. And even if the room had been alive with the grotesque creatures, they'd have been about the least of our worries.

Rasnitov and Preston walked quickly across to the bed, where the blankets had not moved. Mr Prophecy was lying exactly as he had been when we were there earlier.

'At last,' Rasnitov breathed. He reached out and whipped off the top blanket to reveal the figure beneath.

Or rather, the object. Now, I'm not an expert – not then and not since. But I knew at once what the cold, oval, heavy gunmetal object was.

'Oh my –' Barbara Aitken's hand was over her mouth, her eyes wide with horror. 'How did you – why did you . . .' She couldn't form the questions, her mind unable to cope with the magnitude of it. She turned quickly towards the door, but found Krasny standing in the way, his pistol aimed straight at her.

'Now, Mr Preston, Dr Aitken,' Rasnitov said as he leaned over the atom bomb lying on the bed, 'perhaps one of you would be good enough to prime the detonator.'

'But how did it get here?' Barbara Aitken gasped. 'Did you know that was here?' she accused Colin Preston. 'Did you?'

'If you have quite finished,' Rasnitov said coldly. 'Either you prime the device or I shall have Krasny shoot you.'

'Well, since you're going to blow us all to kingdom come anyway,' Dr Aitken started, surprisingly defiant now she had got over the initial shock.

'Enough!' Rasnitov roared. 'I have the papers and plans you brought. I think your usefulness is at an end.'

Krasny smiled and raised his pistol.

102

'No!' Preston shouted, and stepped between them. 'Leave her alone,' he said. 'I'll do it – just leave her alone.'

Dr Aitken was shaking her head. 'Colin – you can't.'

'I must,' he said sadly. 'And maybe, in the long term, it's for the best.'

Anna was holding my arm. 'What do we do? We can't let them explode the bomb.'

That was a conclusion I'd already come to. 'Let's stop things for a while and think about this.'

Our options were limited but surely we could sabotage the atom bomb – perhaps we could age one of the components to the point where it wouldn't work, or something.

Anna's grip on my arm tightened. 'Wait – look.'

My hand was on my time dial, ready to stop events in their tracks. But Anna was pointing at the bomb lying on the bed. The air round it was shimmering like a heat haze and, screwing my eyes up, I could see why. Just visible, sitting astride the bomb, was a Skitter. Its eyes glinted nastily as it stared back at us. Perhaps we were as indistinct and blurred to the creature as it was to us. But it knew we were there.

And it wasn't the only one. Another gargoyle-like face peered round the end of the bomb. Eyes gleamed under the bed. I was aware of a background of chittering, snickering laughter. They'd never let us near the bomb. If we stopped time, they'd be on us in a nano-second.

Oblivious to the creatures, Colin Preston knelt down in front of the bomb and carefully removed a panel on the side. I could see him working carefully at the mechanism inside.

'Set it to go off in . . .' Rasnitov paused and turned to Krasny. They had a rapid conversation in Russian before Rasnitov turned back. 'Four hours should be ample. That gives Krasny two hours to get there and two hours to get back.'

'Where's he going?' I wondered out loud – at the same time as Preston himself asked the same question.

'Since you ask, he is taking our friend Mr Prophecy on a little journey. But before he does that I think we can lose the ladies.'

Preston straightened up abruptly. 'You can't—'

Rasnitov held up his hand. 'Please. I am not a barbarian.'

'Says the man about to set off a nuclear bomb,' I muttered.

'Put them in the cellar with Mr Chowdry,' Rasnitov told Krasny. 'Then come back here.'

Diane Chowdry was horrified. 'But you can't – you promised . . .'

'We will all be in the shelter soon,' Rasnitov told her. 'My promise has not changed.' He smiled, teeth glinting sharply beneath his beard. 'But I imagine you and your husband will have much to talk about.'

'The shelter won't be much use,' Preston said as he worked on the bomb. 'If this goes off right above it, there'll be nothing left but ashes.'

'I'm also not a fool,' Rasnitov said. He had produced a gun of his own – small but deadly – and was pointing it at Preston. 'Please, do not try to tamper with the mechanism or sabotage it. I understand enough of how the thing works to know if you try anything. If you do, then I shall shoot everyone before priming the bomb myself.'

'And if you get it wrong?'

Rasnitov shrugged. 'I'd rather not. But it will serve the same purpose. My life is irrelevant, as is yours. But I would prefer that Krasny move the bomb to a safe distance before it goes off.'

'Safe?' Preston laughed. 'It's still a nuclear bomb. It will still kill thousands. Maybe hundreds of thousands. You know how many people died as a result of the atomic bomb being dropped on Hiroshima?'

'I do,' Rasnitov told him. 'And it was fewer than died as a result of the fire-bombing of Tokyo. You want an end to the threat of nuclear annihilation? So do I.'

'You've got a funny way of going about it.'

'Not really. Krasny will leave the device in the woodland right outside a US air base just under two hours' drive from here. When it explodes . . . Well, I'm sure you can work it out.'

I couldn't. Neither could Anna from the puzzled look she gave me.

But Preston saw it at once. 'A nuclear explosion apparently at a US base, with no warning

– no incoming missile. Everyone will assume it was an accident.'

'That's right. And the result will be an insistence that all American bases be closed, their weapons removed from British soil. Opposition to the nuclear arms race will gain momentum and the West will disarm. I am sure the Soviet Union will then follow suit. How could we not?'

I could tell from the way he said it that he didn't actually believe the Russians would disarm. Why should they? They'd have won.

'You see,' Rasnitov went on, making it sound very reasonable, 'we are making the world a safer place.'

'But people will die!' Preston said.

'Not nearly as many as would die in a nuclear war. President Truman dropped the atom bombs on Japan because he knew that ultimately it would save many more lives. He killed no more people than a few extra raids on Tokyo would have done, but he stopped the war. Is what I am doing now really any different?'

Preston straightened up. 'You're mad,' he said. 'Completely insane. I won't do it.'

'Then I shall shoot you,' Rasnitov said. 'The bomb *will* go off, one way or another. You can be safe in the shelter below us, or dead up here – shot down or blown up. It's your choice.'

It was a hard choice. But Preston made it. He was a braver man than either Anna or I realised at the time as we followed him and Rasnitov down to the cellar.

Krasny was waiting by the door, and he and Rasnitov nattered away in Russian for a few moments. I guess they were deciding to lock everyone down in the shelter, then carry the bomb out to the car. It was big and I was sure it was heavy – could the two of them manage it? Was there a driver or maybe more henchmen waiting outside to help?

Come to that, I wondered how the bomb had got there. Something that Diane Chowdry had arranged, but how she'd done it was anyone's guess. I suppose we could have whizzed back to see, but somehow that didn't seem so important right now.

'How's this going to end?' Anna wondered.

'I'm not sure I want to guess.'

We followed Colin Preston down into the cellar – well, we could always get out again by winding time back or forward to a point where the door was no longer locked.

'Maybe it'll be all right,' I said hopefully. 'Maybe they'll get caught or the bomb won't go off or something.'

'Take a look?' Anna said.

'Got to be better than waiting around here,' I agreed.

Anything would be better than that. Chowdry was sitting on the top bunk, staring at the floor. His wife was sat on the floor as far away from him as possible, close to the periscope. Preston was pacing up and down, lost in his own thoughts, and Barbara Aitken was lying on the bottom bunk, crying quietly into a soggy handkerchief.

All of them, in their own way, waiting for the world to end. Not with a whimper, but with a bang.

'Go forward one day?' I suggested.

'Could be the last day,' Anna said.

In fact we just went forward four hours and a bit for luck. Luck? Whatever. Just into the next day . . .

Colin Preston was standing alone by the periscope. He looked tired and pale. His expression was empty – not just blank but actually lacking. It lacked the slightest hint of emotion, it lacked any sense of hope.

He pressed a button on the side of the periscope and the large, grey, metal cylinder rose slowly until the small window at the bottom was level with Preston's eyes. Preston stared at it, his expression not changing. After several moments he drew in a deep breath, stepped forward and looked through the glass window.

The periscope turned as Preston walked slowly round with it, checking 360 degrees. My guess was that whatever he was looking at, it wasn't a room in the house above.

But as soon as he stepped away, I stopped time.

Like Preston, both Anna and I paused before going to the periscope. We looked at each other, we looked at Preston – his face, if anything, even emptier than before. Then, finally, I nodded to Anna and she stepped up to the periscope.

Time did not flicker, but it still seemed an eternity before she stepped back. A single tear ran down her cheek and she turned away.

The window was shaped like a pair of binoculars. A figure 8 on its side. The symbol for infinity – ∞. Would I look out onto infinity?

I looked out onto nothing. Emptiness. Wasteland. It was a desert – flat, featureless, grey. Maybe because it was so stark, so lacking in character, I got the impression I had seen it before. The broken remains of a tree struggled through the dust like a child's stick-painting. The sky was the colour of gunmetal, the colour of the bomb.

I stepped away and felt Anna's arm round my shoulder.

'We have to go back,' she said. 'We have to stop this.'

I nodded, not sure I could speak. I'll never forget the barren emptiness of what I saw that day

– no matter whether it was really the past, the present or the future. I'll never forget the feel of the single tear that ran down my cheek.

I reached for my time dial and we returned to the day before – and the sound of gunfire.

CHAPTER NINE

🕐 SUNDAY 11TH SEPTEMBER 1955

We remained a split second in the future of what was going on. Invisible, in effect, to the people in the cellar shelter. But we could see and hear everything that was happening: the shouts, the gunfire, the rattle of the door above being unlocked.

'We've jumped ahead a bit,' I realised.

We'd come back a few minutes after we left and it seemed that events had moved along.

'What's happening?' Anna wondered as there was another burst of gunfire. Something heavy clattered on the top steps.

'Let's go back and find out,' I said.

We didn't have to wind time back far – just to the point where the door was opened for Krasny and Rasnitov to put Colin Preston in the cellar. We'd sneaked in with him and now we sneaked out again at the same time. We'd have passed ourselves on the way, if we'd really been there at all.

'So let's see what happens next,' I said to Anna.

'You think Rasnitov and Krasny were doing the shooting?' she asked as we stood in the hall, waiting to see what would occur.

'Not all of it. Wrong sort of guns. There was machine-gun fire in there too.'

'Was there? Must be a boy thing.'

'Won't be long and we'll find out what's happening.'

'It's to do with Lewis,' Anna said. She's so much brighter and quicker than me sometimes.

'How do you mean? He's not here any more. Never was. Time changed so he was never here.'

She nodded. 'That's right. Remember, back in that office? The man with the pipe – the man in charge – he said he had no one he could send in undercover or whatever.'

'Because Lewis doesn't exist any more. So what's about to happen is whatever action that man took instead of sending Lewis – his alternative plan.'

'Could be,' Anna said. 'We'll soon find out.'

We paused to watch a black car draw up in front of the house. Outside it was dark and it was raining, but we could see the silhouette of the driver as he got out. Another man – huge and hulking – emerged from the back of the car and they came into the house.

'Goons,' I said.

'What?'

'Henchmen, hired help. Bodyguards or something.'

We watched them dripping on the marble floor. One of them shouted in Russian and Rasnitov's voice answered from upstairs.

'Calling them to help with the bomb, probably,' Anna said as the two of them made their way ponderously up the stairs.

'That's how they'll get it into the car and out again,' I agreed. 'While Rasnitov stays safe and sound here.'

'Until the pipe-smoking man's friends arrive,' Anna said. 'That's what I was telling you.'

I remembered. 'That woman was calling someone to send in a team.'

'And I'll bet you they'll be here any minute now,' Anna said. 'Whoever got rid of Lewis has messed it up. They'd have been better to keep him here and lock him up like Chowdry.'

'Diane Chowdry's to blame, I'd guess,' I said. 'She noticed someone had been searching, remember? She sent Lewis up to see Mr Prophecy.'

'But Mr Prophecy is a bomb.'

'Mr Prophecy is some sort of paradox,' I told her. 'An impossibility. A bomb – a cataclysmic event – that might or might not go off. That might be what happened to Lewis. he got too close to the paradox, to the hole it makes in time – between reality and unreality. And he fell through it. He just fell out of reality.'

'Or he was pushed by one of the Skitters. Mrs Chowdry probably didn't even know what she was doing when she sent him up there. She just knew it was a way of getting rid of him when he started to ask questions and search the house.'

116

Anna had a point. There was a controlling force behind all this. Someone or something we hadn't encountered yet, who'd told Diane Chowdry what to do . . .

More cars were arriving. The Russian heavies had left the front door open and we heard the powerful motors above the insistent sound of the rain. Then tyres crunched loudly on the gravel of the drive outside as the cars skidded to an urgent halt.

'There's something else, something more than we're seeing. Someone controlling events here – and it isn't Rasnitov.'

'Not any more, it isn't,' Anna agreed.

Men in dark combat uniforms were running into the house. We stepped back to let them though, though of course they hadn't seen us. They were wearing masks that covered their faces, leaving just darkened eyes visible.

The first man waved for others to move ahead of him. There were eight of them in all, moving forward in waves. Four would take up position, sheltering behind a grandfather clock or under the stairs. Then the next four would move ahead, while their colleagues covered them. All were carrying sub-machine guns – large and clunky compared with what I'd seen on TV. But brutal and deadly even so.

I put the sudden queasy feeling I was getting down to the excitement, the surprise, the adrenaline. I should have known better. Anna and I watched as the slow motion gun battle played out. We'd slowed it down in case we needed to join in.

I don't mean we'd be snatching up guns and blazing away. But we might need to nudge some-one one way or the other, to make sure the right side won. We thought.

There were shouts from upstairs – slurred, slow, deep, Russian. A masked gunman close to me was knocked backwards by a bullet. He crashed into the grandfather clock and slumped impossibly slowly to the ground. The clock wobbled dangerously, and on instinct I put out a hand into real, normal time and steadied it.

Down the corridor that led to the kitchens I could see Krasny crouching, holding his pistol. I'd assumed he was upstairs with Rasnitov and the other heavies. I'd been wrong. Now he was opening the door to the cellar. It slammed slowly closed behind him, bullet holes stitching across the wooden panelling.

'Upstairs,' I said to Anna.

'What about Krasny?'

'We can wind back and see what he's up to.'

She was worried about her father. 'No – Krasny first!'

I pulled her round and stared into her eyes – we're about the same height. We were then. 'Krasny doesn't have an atom bomb.'

Anna blinked, then nodded. I'm sure it was a hard decision, but she didn't hesitate. Well, you know she wouldn't.

We ran up the stairs. The attacking gunmen were hurrying too, but we streaked past them. To us, they were moving incredibly slowly.

There were two of the Russian bodyguards on the landing. One was hurled back and smashed into the wall as we approached. I think the burst of gunfire from the man on the stairs actually went right through me, but I can't be sure. It didn't matter.

The second man backed quickly away down the passage. Behind him I could see that the door to Mr Prophecy's room – the room with the bomb – was standing open.

It slammed shut before he reached it. The man scrabbled at the handle, shouting and yelling and hammering on the door. Then he sank slowly to the floor as the gunmen raced slowly towards him.

We went through Barbara Aitken's room. The connecting door was locked, but I simply moved it to a point in time when it wasn't and we went through.

Rasnitov was standing by the bomb. He had the inspection panel open in its side and was fiddling with the mechanism. Didn't take rocket – or atomic – science to work out what he was up to. As far as he knew he was probably dead already. And if an atom bomb went off fifty or a hundred or however many miles away from where it was supposed to . . . Well, as far as he was concerned the effect and the consequences would most likely be the same anyhow.

'We have to stop him,' Anna said.

And we could have. I'm sure we could have. Pretty sure. Almost. As things turned out, though, we didn't have to.

Rasnitov seemed to sense we were there, even though he couldn't have seen or heard us. Or perhaps he just felt what was happening to him. He turned, and his face was lined with age. His cheeks were flabby, his jaw less firm. His hair whitened as we watched.

And the Skitters guarding the bomb laughed and chattered as they emerged from behind it to watch.

An aged hand reached desperately for the bomb mechanism. But the flesh withered and rotted before Rasnitov got there. He stared at the dry sticks that had been his fingers. His face was the same – staring sockets for eyes, pale bone where there had been flesh and skin and beard. Then the skeleton collapsed to the floor, crumbling to dust. Even the dust was decaying, fading, disappearing.

By the time the door crashed open and several masked gunmen rushed into the room, there was nothing left.

Time was running at normal speed again, although Anna and I were not inside it. It froze as the lead gunman pulled out a radio handset. And we were running for the cellar.

'Can't wind it back,' I gasped. 'If I did it might give Rasnitov another chance.'

'Why did the Skitters stop him?'

I was wondering the same thing myself. I didn't have an answer. But my blood ran cold as Anna suggested one.

'Unless they need the bomb themselves. For something else.'

'But what?' I asked.

The cellar door was closed and locked. We wound time forward rather than back, then froze it. Paused reality. We dived down the stairs, almost falling over ourselves and each other.

Krasny was standing immobile – frozen in time like everyone else. He was pointing his gun at Colin Preston and Gerald Chowdry. Barbara Aitken and Diane Chowdry were both at the back of the room, looking scared.

'Hostages,' I said. 'He's locked them all down

122

here. No one can get in from outside, at least not easily.'

'You think he'll demand they let him go?'

'Or just shoot everyone.'

'Charming,' Anna muttered. 'Better stop him, then.'

'Better had.'

It would have been simplest to take the gun off Krasny while he was frozen. But it doesn't work like that. Time has a way of compensating if you try to change things. Like sending the troops in when Lewis disappeared. Like maybe Krasny would have another gun or a knife. It's better to change events as they move forward rather than try to cheat.

So the best option was a distraction. Krasny had no idea we were there. When time started up again with Anna and I standing either side of him it seemed as if we'd just suddenly appeared. Somehow. His mind would have rationalised it – he'd have thought we'd sneaked up behind him or something. If he'd had time.

'Hi there,' I said.

He visibly jumped. Hardly surprising.

Then Anna said, from behind him. 'How do you do?'

Krasny spun round, the gun ready. But then it was flying from his hand as Colin Preston kicked out violently and sent it flying. His fist smacked into Krasny's face. Krasny was knocked backwards. There was a cry – but it was from Preston, nursing his bruised knuckles.

'Oh – that looks easier in the movies,' he complained, shaking his hand in pain.

'Don't try it at home, children,' I murmured.

Chowdry had recovered the gun and was aiming it at Krasny. 'Where did you two spring from?' he asked.

'Oh, we were hiding down here,' I said.

'Keeping away from the shooting,' Anna added.

It wasn't a very plausible explanation but it would have to do. There was no time for them to ask for details or point out there was actually nowhere we could have been hiding. Because at that moment we all heard the door at the top of the stairs swing open. It creaked heavily on the hinges, damaged perhaps by the gunfire. Booted feet on the stairs.

'How did they get in?' Anna asked.

'Duplicate key?' I offered. Then suddenly, I knew. My stomach convulsed, and even before the first Skitter scurried down the stairs and into the shelter, I knew exactly how they'd got it. 'No,' I gasped. 'They did it the same way we did.'

Anna stared at me aghast. 'But that would mean . . .'

There were several Skitters gathered at the foot of the stairs, rocking from side to side as they surveyed the scene in the shelter. They were itching to attack someone – anyone – I could see it in their eyes.

Three gunmen arrived behind them. Two were carrying machine guns, while their leader held a pistol.

'Cellar secured, sir,' one of the gunmen said.

'I can see that, thank you,' the leader said.

Colin Preston breathed an audible sigh of relief. Despite the balaclava mask, he'd recognised the man's voice. 'It's you – thank goodness you're here at last. I was getting worried.'

'Who are these people?' Chowdry asked. He

was still holding Krasny's gun, but Preston took it from him.

'They're from the security service. I've been working with them to flush out the traitors, and to tip Rasnitov's hand. Though we almost went too far.' He nodded to the leading gunman. 'This is Mr Blackler, from MI5 Operations.'

But it wasn't. I knew it wasn't and so did Anna. Mr Blackler reached up with his free hand and pulled off the mask. The face that was revealed beneath was one both Anna and I knew very well. Knew and feared.

It was Darkling Midnight.

The soldiers (or agents, or whatever they actually were) led everyone from the shelter, keeping Krasny, Diane Chowdry and Barbara Aitken under close watch. Everyone, that is, except for me and Anna.

I'd been frantically trying to get my time dial to work and I could see Anna doing the same. But without effect – Midnight has a way of suppressing their power, stopping them from working. As I've told you, sometimes I can make things happen anyway, things with time I mean. But it's a sort of raw power, untamed. I couldn't control it then.

Finally everyone else was on their way up the

127

stairs. Anna and I made to follow, but Midnight stepped in front of us, blocking the way.

'Leaving so soon?'

It was strange seeing him in a combat uniform rather than the more theatrical get-up he usually prefers – cape and hat and cane. But if anything it made him seem more dangerous. He certainly didn't need the gun, but he was holding it anyway. Skitters blurred and flickered in and out of existence around him.

'Things to do,' I told him, trying to sound confident and defiant. 'You've stopped the bomb going off, but there are still a few things we need to sort out.'

'I didn't stop the bomb going off,' he said, smiling thinly. 'You have Colin Preston to thank for that.'

'What do you mean?' Anna demanded.

Midnight was backing up the stairs. 'Yes, despite your fears and anxieties, it turns out your father is a hero after all.'

'Wait,' I said. 'You can't just leave us down here.'

'Oh yes, I can.'

I ran to the steps.

'Think you can stop a bullet?' Midnight said. He sounded amused at the idea. 'Well, perhaps you can. Only one way to find out, isn't there? And I'm more than happy to put it to the test, you know.'

I felt Anna's hand on my shoulder, holding me back. 'We can get out,' she whispered. 'The time corridor, remember.'

She was right. Even without our time dials working, we could get into the time corridor, and from that out into another period of history far enough away from Midnight that the dials would work and we could go where we wanted. I held back and let Midnight disappear up the stairs.

'Don't worry,' he called down to us. 'You won't be alone for long. Mr Prophecy will be coming to keep you company. And someone else of course. The person I need to rearm the bomb.'

Then the door clanged shut, leaving us alone in the shelter.

'What's he up to?' Anna asked quietly.

'I don't know. But the sooner we get out of here the better.'

We went over to the wall where the time corridor had been. Even as we approached, I could feel . . . nothing. No tingling trepidation, no sense of the power of time itself . . .

'It's gone,' Anna realised. 'He's turned it off.'

'Can he do that?' I was desperately prodding at the wall, but without any success.

'Obviously he can. Since he put it here, he can take it away again.'

'So why was it here in the first place?'

'Once it's set up he can turn it on and off. He needs it later, but not right now I'm guessing.'

'Like putting in an electric light? You need to go to the trouble of wiring it all up but that doesn't mean you want it switched on all the time.'

'Exactly.'

'I guess we have to wait here then.' I went and sat on the bottom bunk. I wasn't used to having to wait.

'Let's hope it's not for long,' Anna said as she sat down beside me.

'Let's hope the world doesn't end while we're waiting,' I told her.

*

Actually we didn't have to wait long. Colin Preston was ushered back into the shelter by 'Mr Blackler' and seemed surprised to see us. But 'Mr Blackler' waved him away and muttered something to Preston about 'need to know' and security.

Preston was distracted at that point, anyway, as Mr Prophecy joined us, just as Midnight had promised. Two soldiers, now without their balaclava masks, carefully carried the heavy bomb down into the shelter and put it gingerly on the floor.

Midnight opened the inspection hatch in the side where Rasnitov had been trying to set it off and where earlier Preston had apparently primed the bomb.

'You removed the trigger fuse,' Midnight said to Preston.

'It seemed like a good idea. Otherwise that lunatic might actually have set the thing off.'

'And we can't have that,' Midnight agreed. He held out his hand. 'I'll take it now, please. The fuse.'

'Don't give it to him,' Anna blurted.

'No, don't,' I agreed. Like that would help.

Preston looked at us, frowning.

'They're just children,' Midnight said. 'I'll see they are looked after.' I didn't like the way he said 'looked after' but Preston nodded, as if satisfied.

'Maybe I should hold on to the fuse, though, all the same,' he said.

Anna and I breathed audible sighs of relief.

'Maybe you should follow orders,' Midnight told him.

Preston hesitated. But then he took a thin cylinder of metal from his jacket pocket and held it out to Midnight. 'You're not going to put it back, Mr Blackler?' he checked.

Midnight's smile was as false as his alias. 'Of course not. It will be quite safe.'

I leaped to my feet, Anna close behind me. And a Skitter broke out of the air in front of us, its nasty little eyes gleaming excitedly. I glanced at the sharp claws, poised ready to rip into us. And I sat down again. I could see other Skitters grouped round the bomb – too many for me and Anna to take on, even if my power over time decided to work.

Midnight smiled amiably at us, then led Preston to the stairs. 'Thank you so much for all your help. Rest assured it hasn't gone unnoticed. Someone will be in touch, but right now Sanders will drive you back to London.'

Together they walked up the stairs.

Midnight paused and looked back at us. From upstairs we could hear the grandfather clock in the hall chiming the hour. 'It's midnight,' he said. 'How appropriate, don't you think?' Then he turned and followed Preston from the cellar.

🕐 MONDAY 12TH SEPTEMBER 1955

In less than a minute, Midnight was back.

'You're going to set the bomb off, aren't you?' Anna accused.

'Yes.'

The simplicity of his answer shocked me. One simple little word that meant so much – the end of everything. Though I didn't realise how literally true that was. I couldn't see past the nuclear explosion or understand what would happen to us, the war that might follow – or at the very least the devastation to history as I knew it. Would my parents survive? Would my sister, Ellie, ever even exist?

'You're mad,' I said. It didn't sound very effective or helpful. But what else can you say?

'The time corridor is still here,' Midnight said. I thought maybe he was offering us a way out, a means of escape. But in fact he was gloating. 'I just shifted the entrance to it a little behind that wall. The other side of the steel plates and lead lining. A shame,' he went on, though he didn't sound at all sad about it. 'Otherwise you could simply have climbed through and walked away.'

'Like you?' I said. 'Blow up a chunk of Britain and just walk away?'

'Oh, please.' He sounded insulted. 'This isn't about blowing up Britain. It's about the end of the world.'

He knelt down and pushed the metal fuse Preston had given him into the bomb mechanism.

I could see a row of numerals – a counter. It was set to 500, and as we watched it clicked over to 499.

'No!' I yelled, and hurled myself across the room at Midnight. At once the air was alive with Skitters – and with Midnight's caustic laughter. The Skitters held me tight as I thrashed and fought. I could see Anna close beside me – also caught.

One of the Skitters holding me exploded into fragments. Another crumbled to dust. In a few moments I would be free.

'Stop that!' Midnight ordered.

'No!' I screamed back at him.

A third Skitter seemed to weather, its features flaking away like old stone.

'Stop now,' Midnight said, 'or my Skitters will kill Anna.'

Well, I had no choice. Stop a nuclear explosion or save Anna. No contest. Even though we'd both die anyway – no contest. And I was so ashamed, not just that I couldn't let her die to save the world, but that Midnight knew it.

*

135

It seemed as though we sat for ever on the bunk in that cellar. Neither of us said anything. I suppose I was sulking. Anna put her arm round my shoulder, but she couldn't bring herself to tell me I'd done the right thing. Had I done the right thing?

So we sat there and we watched the numbers click down, unable to stop them or slow them or wind them back the other way. Midnight was gone, but he had left several Skitters behind. They chattered away to each other, grey tongues licking grey lips as they anticipated the moment when the countdown would reach zero. A couple of them scampered round the bomb as if playing a bizarre game of tag. Another was sitting on top of it, watching its fellows through gleaming red eyes.

'There comes a point,' I said at last, 'when the only thing we can do is fight our way past the Skitters and pull out wires, hoping we can defuse the thing.'

'And if you just set the bomb off?'

'It's going to go off anyway.'

'Someone might come.'

136

'Or they might not. And even if they do . . .'

I left the comment hanging in the air while the Skitters continued to circle the bomb.

'We have to wait till the last moment,' Anna said flatly. Her voice was hers, only it wasn't – there was no feeling in it. None of the usual sarcasm or joy or tetchiness or excitement. Empty.

'There comes a point,' I repeated.

'I suppose there does,' she said.

But before the point came, with the numbers clicking round to 347, we heard footsteps on the stairs.

Colin Preston looked pale and afraid. 'Tell me he isn't really doing it,' he said, his voice a husky croak.

'He's doing it,' I said. I pointed at the bomb. 'Unless you can stop it.'

Preston knelt by the bomb, inspecting the mechanism. The Skitter sitting on top watched him with interest but made no attempt to stop him. Not yet. But in a moment it could swipe him away with its clawed hand.

'I thought I was helping,' Preston said as he

examined it. 'Blackler came to me – told me there was a spy in Chowdry's organisation. I thought I was working for him. I sent a message to MI5, like he said. He told me it needed someone on the inside to go to them and make them see sense.'

'So you brought the bomb here too, didn't you?' I said.

The other Skitters had stopped their game and were grouped round Preston. He couldn't see them watching him through their deep-set little eyes. Couldn't feel the movement of air as their wings beat lazily. Couldn't know how close he was to death – or worse. If they got him, he might be lost like us, might never have even existed.

He nodded. 'I arranged for Mrs Chowdry to acquire it.' He leaned back from the mechanism, shaking his head in despair. 'I can't do it,' he said, his voice barely a whisper. 'I don't know how to stop it.'

The Skitter on top of the bomb made a giggling noise and bounced up and down with unpleasant glee. The numbers were at 302.

'Leave it,' I said. 'We'll think of something.'

The Skitters were getting more interested in Preston and I didn't want to lose him too. I didn't want him ripped apart or tossed out of reality by those spiteful creatures.

'Why did you trust him?' Anna asked Preston. She still sounded empty.

'I didn't. I didn't trust him at all, but he told me I had to help. I convinced myself it was for the best, but that isn't why I brought Barbara here, that isn't why we brought the plans and . . .' His body shuddered. 'And this.'

'Then – why?' I asked.

But I was beginning to guess, beginning to work it out. I clutched Anna's hand and held it tight.

'Once I'd started, I tried to stop. I said I wouldn't do it – wouldn't come here. That MI5 must have enough by now, they didn't need me, and they certainly didn't need the bomb. But he told me – Blackler told me such incredible things.'

'About time?'

He nodded, turning from the bomb to look at us. I could see the tears running down the man's crumpled face. 'I didn't believe him, but he showed me . . . Down here – he showed me . . .'

'It's all right,' Anna said. 'We saw it too. The time corridor.'

'A good description,' he agreed.

'But that isn't why you brought the bomb here, why you arranged for Midnight – I mean Blackler – to get control of it,' I said.

Preston shook his head. 'He told me . . . I don't know – I don't remember. How can that be possible? How can it be true and I don't even know? We tried so hard. Me and Mary. If she knew – if she thought it was even possible . . . That we'd lost . . .'

I felt Anna tense at the sound of Preston's wife's name. A name she must know so well. Behind him the Skitters were leaning forward too – listening, amused.

'What did Midnight tell you?' she said. There was emotion in her voice now. More emotion than could be expressed. 'What did he tell you was *lost*?'

Preston looked at her, more tears welling up in his eyes. 'He told me I had a daughter,' Anna's father said. 'And that – even though I don't know it, even though I can't remember her – if I helped him, I would see her again.'

Anna lapsed into a stunned, brooding silence. I guess it was bad enough that she felt I'd given up a chance to save the world because of her. Now she'd discovered her dad had helped bring the world to the brink of disaster because of her too. And he didn't even know she had ever existed.

So it was up to me to explain. Well, not the whole father–daughter thing. That was between them. They'd get round to it eventually – if we all lived that long.

'The man you call Mr Blackler we know as Midnight,' I said. 'We don't have a lot of time . . .' I glanced at the numbers on the bomb – now down to 217 . . . 'but basically he isn't a

142

nice guy. He's . . . Well, he's trying to destroy the world. He thinks that is a good thing, that he and his colleagues can rebuild a better one in its place. But we're not convinced and we were sent here – at this time – to stop him.'

The countdown clicked to 213.

'We're not doing all that well at the moment,' I admitted.

Preston was frowning. 'Destroy the world? But this bomb won't do that. It won't spark a retaliation. As Rasnitov said, it might force Britain to remove the US nukes, even though it means a lot of people will die. Including us. But it's relatively low yield. It won't destroy that much.'

'Midnight said it will destroy the world,' Anna said. 'He doesn't lie.'

Actually he lies all the time and we both knew it. But about something like this? Nope, I was with Anna. Preston didn't believe it – though the three of us were going to die anyway. In 202 seconds. But perhaps a vision of the future might focus his mind and spur him on to find a way past the Skitters to stop the bomb.

'I'll show you,' I said.

Anna frowned. 'Can you?'

'Maybe.' To be honest, I didn't know. But the periscope was there. I'd seen what Preston had seen through it – what he would see through it. It obviously wasn't going to happen after the explosion because neither Preston nor the periscope would be here then. Midnight's influence meant that I couldn't move time forwards or backwards – I'd been concentrating on stopping the countdown clock with no effect I could see at all. Maybe I'd stretched the seconds out by a few tenths of a second here and there. But nothing very useful. Midnight was too close and too powerful.

So I couldn't change the way time was working. But maybe I could use something that was already there. The time corridor Midnight had set up (and why did he do that? A voice asked quietly in the back of my mind – what's it really for?) was tantalisingly close. Not so we could climb into it and walk to another point in history. But perhaps close enough for me to nudge a periscope into it. So it showed this same place, but in another time.

Preston followed me over to the periscope. 'I'll just see the room above,' he said.

'Try it.'

The time corridor stopped in the present. There was nothing further forward in the future – maybe because there really was no future and this was going to be the end of everything. I tried not to think about that. Instead I thought back to when Anna and I were in the corridor – the scenes we had witnessed. And I remembered where I had seen that devastated landscape Anna and I had looked at through the periscope. *When* I had seen it.

Preston looked tired and pale. His expression was empty – not just blank but actually lacking. It lacked the slightest hint of emotion; it lacked any sense of hope.

He pressed a button on the side of the periscope and the large, grey, metal cylinder rose slowly until the small window at the bottom was level with Preston's eyes. Preston stared at it, his expression not changing. After several moments he drew in a deep breath, stepped forward and looked through the glass window.

The periscope turned as Preston walked slowly round with it, checking 360 degrees. I knew that he wasn't simply looking at a room in the house above. He was seeing something else. When he stepped away, Preston's face was, if anything, even emptier than before.

This was the moment we had experienced earlier, Anna and I. This was the time we had come forward to, when we had looked through the periscope ourselves. So, even though I couldn't tell they were there, I waited long enough for that Anna and I from the day before to have stopped time and looked for ourselves. Then I stepped forward to take Preston's place at the periscope and looked again. Only this time I knew what I was looking at.

The emptiness, the wasteland. It was a desert – flat, featureless, grey. The broken remains of a tree struggled through the dust like a child's stick-painting. The sky was the colour of gun-metal, the colour of the bomb. But I knew now that it was not a vision of the future. It was an image of the past – the distant past. Millions of years even before the dinosaurs. Plucked out of the time corridor and put here to persuade Preston he had to do something. *Anything.* Would it work? Or had I just depressed and broken him?

'We have to stop this,' Preston said with renewed determination.

'Yes, we do,' I agreed. 'But it isn't as easy as it looks.'

'It doesn't look easy at all,' Preston said. 'If I pull out the wrong wire we'll just set the bomb off early.'

Anna and I looked at each other. 'There's something else,' Anna said. 'Something you can't see.'

'Several somethings,' I explained. 'Four, actually. Creatures. Like imps or demons. Anna and I will try to hold them back.'

I looked at Anna for agreement. The Skitters would kill us if they could. And they probably could.

She took a deep breath, then nodded.

The numbers were at 156.

'I can't see anything,' Preston said, shaking his head.

'Believe me, they're there. You'll see them if they want you to.'

The Skitters were ready for us. I had no idea – still have no idea – if they can understand us. Perhaps all they hear when we speak is garbled noises like they seem to make. Though Midnight can communicate with them.

'You'll die with us when the bomb goes off,' I told them. 'Why don't you escape while you can, or let us defuse it?' I adjusted the flat black disc on my wrist that was my dial and again tried to slow or stop time. But it still didn't work. Did that mean that Midnight wasn't far away? I was sure he'd leave before the bomb went off. But if it was, like, a millisecond before I'd never catch the moment.

And it's all very well stopping time, but what if you can never start it again without destroying the world? Would this bomb destroy the world? How did that work? My mind was spinning round the same thoughts and questions.

So it was almost a relief to focus on something else, even if it was another problem, another whole set of questions.

Preston had paused, halfway to the bomb, with

148

Anna and I beside him. He could see it too, I realised.

We all could – we could all see Anna, a ghostly, ethereal Anna being dragged out of the cellar by a group of Skitters.

'Are those the creatures you meant?'

I nodded.

'But . . . they're like ghosts. And they've got . . .' Preston turned to Anna in surprise. 'They've got you.'

'It isn't real,' she told him. 'I don't know what it is, but it isn't real. It's the future, or the past. A past that maybe never happened. A might-have-been.'

As she said it things clicked into place. 'Of course.' The ghostly image was already fading, but I knew what it was now. 'That's exactly what we saw – here and upstairs. It's how events would have played out, what would have happened if you hadn't been lost, Anna.'

'Lost?' Preston said. 'Who's lost? What do you mean?'

'Lost in time,' I said. 'Taken out of reality. Never was.'

'You mean . . .' Anna was frowning as she struggled to work it out. 'You mean, if I hadn't been lost, then this was how Midnight would persuade . . .' She hesitated and glanced at her father. 'How he'd persuade Mr Preston to help him?'

'The threat. You were – or rather would have been – locked up down here. Then dragged off and lost if Mr Preston didn't agree to help. Like Lewis was. Maybe that's actually what happened, once. In another time. But certainly, this is how it might have been if . . .'

Preston interrupted me: 'If I'd had a daughter,' he said. 'Is that it?'

I looked at Anna. She looked at Preston. 'Yes,' she said, and there was a whole world of emotion behind that one little word. 'If you'd had a daughter. But you never did. It never happened. And now we have to stop the bomb.'

The numbers clicked over to 97. But Preston wasn't watching them. He was staring at Anna. He reached out his hand and gently stoked her cheek. She didn't stop him, but I saw her lip was trembling as he touched her.

'It's you, isn't it?' Preston said quietly. 'Blackler – Midnight, he promised. Did he keep that promise? That one promise? The most important promise? Is it you?'

Anna couldn't answer. But she nodded, his hand still against her cheek.

'Anna,' Preston said, 'is such a lovely name. It's the name we always knew we'd give our daughter.'

And he hugged her tight.

As they both cried.

As I stood alone in the cellar.

And the numbers on the bomb ticked closer to the end of the world.

In those endless last few seconds, all I could do was think. I thought about Anna and her father. About my own parents and my sister, Ellie. About the end of the world and what Midnight could be planning.

I thought about how the time corridor was just behind a thin metal plate on the other side of the room, and if only it were a centimetre or two closer Anna and Preston and I could just walk away. And I wondered if, really, we could. If we *would*.

And then I realised why the time corridor was there, and what Midnight's plan actually was, and I went totally cold.

'We have to stop this now!'

The numbers were on 53.

Anna pulled away reluctantly from her father.

'I know what he's doing,' I told her. 'It's the time corridor. If we don't stop the bomb, the explosion will rip through that wall.'

'Well, of course it will,' she said. But even as she said it, her expression darkened as she realised what I was telling her. 'Into the time corridor.'

'And out through every portal – every window and doorway into other times. Just like we could step through into other times, so can the bomb. The explosion won't just happen here and now, it will happen at every point in history. It will destroy . . . everything.'

'A blank canvas,' Anna said. 'The end of history, so he can start again and build it how he wants it.'

I don't know if Preston had any idea what we were talking about, but he nodded grimly and walked purposefully towards the bomb.

At once the air was alive with thrashing Skitters. Preston stepped back in surprise as one nipped at him. Another slashed at his face, and Anna ran forward to knock the claw aside.

I joined her and together we fought the Skitters, trying to keep them away from Preston as he struggled past the creatures he could barely see to get to the open inspection hatch in the side of the bomb.

46 . . . 45 . . . 44 . . .

I thumped at a Skitter and felt its leathery skin slacken as it aged. Some of my power over time was returning. Did that mean that Midnight was leaving? Or that my anger and determination were finally coming back and breaking through the way Midnight could suppress that power? I didn't stop to worry about it. I held the Skitter tight. It thrashed and clawed and bit. Others were nipping and slashing at me too.

Beside me, Anna's hair was in a whirl as she lashed out at any of the creatures that came close. We'd managed to get between the Skitters and the bomb, allowing Preston to work away at the hatch. I prayed he knew what he was doing. I caught a glimpse of the numbers between the flap of wings and blur of claws: 27.

The far wall was changing, melting away. I could see the corridor stretching out into infinity – a window through all of time. Muddled images overlaid each other as if every point in history was vying for supremacy with every other moment of the past. The wasteland of prehistory; dinosaurs; rolling green English countryside; a Spitfire banking, its distinctive curved wings silhouetted against the blue of the sky.

I knew it wasn't a way of escape now. If we tried to leave, the blast of the bomb would follow us, all through history. We couldn't let it explode while the corridor was open.

15 . . .

Another Skitter shimmered into existence beside the bomb. Preston had his hands right inside the workings, desperately feeling for a wire or component. The Skitter was on him instantly, wings flapping and claws ripping down at him. Forcing him away from the bomb casing.

He struggled to get back to it, his scratched face a mask of determination. But another Skitter appeared from nowhere and dragged him away.

'No!' I yelled, smashing aside a Skitter that flew

at me. It shattered, like brittle stone. A Skitter holding my other arm simply disappeared.

Preston managed – somehow – to break free. He leaped at the bomb, fingers scrabbling across the metal casing as he fumbled for the hatch, Skitters closing in on him.

The countdown reached 10.

I held my breath.

And the countdown was still at 10.

The air around us seemed to thin and grow calm again. Like a storm suddenly dying away to nothing. Anna was lying on the floor, hands over her face to protect it. She peeped out between her fingers.

Preston was frozen at the bomb. The countdown was stopped at 10. And Anna and I were laughing with relief.

'You did it!' I yelled triumphantly.

But Preston didn't move. Not at all. He wasn't even breathing.

'Oh no,' Anna murmured.

And a voice behind us said, 'Actually, it was me.'

We turned and Midnight was standing there.

He was out of combat gear and instead wearing his more usual dark suit and cloak, complete with top hat and silver-tipped cane. The Skitters that had been attacking us were crouched beside him like grotesque pets. He patted one on the head and it gave a low growl like a contented puppy.

'Changed your mind?' I asked. I had to struggle to stop my voice from shaking.

'Hardly. But I thought *you* might have changed your mind, Jamie.'

'What do you mean?'

'It could be your last chance,' Midnight said. 'Ten seconds to decide. Jamie,' he went on, with an enthusiasm that I didn't share, 'just think about it – you could save the world.'

'And how can he do that?' Anna demanded.

'By agreeing to come and work with me.'

I laughed, but it sounded hollow in the silence of the shelter. 'You mean, like, save the world now so I can help you destroy it later.'

'Oh, you might talk me out of it.' He stepped forward, the flippancy and amusement gone. 'My way really is better. Everything I do is for the best.'

'Oh yeah, right,' I said, making no attempt to disguise my sarcasm.

'Join me and you will find out that it is true.'

'Or not,' Anna said.

'Please don't try to talk him out of it, Miss Preston,' Midnight said.

He'd never called her Miss Preston before. In fact, usually he ignored Anna completely. He was only interested in me, or rather the power I was developing. Either he wanted it for his own purposes, or he wanted me out of the way and unable to oppose him. I suppose I should have been flattered he would go to such lengths. But I was too busy being frightened and angry.

'After all,' Midnight went on, 'it's your only hope of ever being reunited with your father, with your family. Of leading a normal, real life.'

Anna looked at her dad, crouched beside the bomb, the countdown still stopped at 10. That was why he'd called her 'Miss Preston' – to remind her of who she really was. Who she might once have been, and could be again. If he was telling the truth.

'Lost is for ever,' Anna said sadly. 'He might

know who I am now, but I'm not his daughter. Not really. How can I be? We've only just met.'

'It's not for ever,' Midnight said. 'I can put you back. You know I can – you've seen me do it.'

Which we had. We'd seen a man called Norman Sellwood taken out of time – lost. Then put back as if he'd never been away, without even knowing what had happened to him. Senex had warned me of the cost – of terrible things that might happen. But I'd seen no sign of that. Just Sellwood, enjoying a normal life as if nothing had happened to him. Because nothing *had* happened to him.

Anna looked at me. Then she looked back at her father. Finally she turned to Midnight. 'How?' she asked quietly.

'It takes tremendous power and the time zones have to be synchronised. If – or perhaps I should say when – the bomb explodes, the power will surge down the time corridor and blast out through every time. It will wipe out everything. Not just this place throughout history. That energy, that break in time, will be enough to rupture and tear apart the whole fragile fabric that holds reality together. We really shall have a blank canvas with which to start again.'

'That doesn't answer her question,' I said.

We couldn't go through with it. I couldn't join Midnight. Not even to save the world. Could I? Was that really what Senex was so afraid of and was warning me against – that cost? But what choice did I have? Midnight had just told me what would happen if I didn't . . . Could I pretend? Or join him for a while, for just long enough to find out who he really worked for and what they were actually up to? I could always leave . . . Well, I knew deep down that almost certainly I couldn't. It was like being lost – join Midnight and it's for ever.

'If I close down the time corridor,' Midnight said, 'then the energy still has to go somewhere.'

'An atomic explosion,' I said.

'But that's so boring. So predictable.'

'What, then?' Anna asked.

'I channel that power and energy, make use of it. With a synchonisation coordinator. That will link this time to other times that are connected.'

'Such as?' I said.

He smiled. 'Such as the moment Anna Preston was lost. The moment she stopped being a hostage locked in this cellar by Diane Chowdry to force her father to work for Rasnitov, and was instead taken by the Skitters to see Mr Prophecy. The very same exact moment, in fact, that the bomb will go off.'

As he said it, while he was still speaking, the ghostly image of Anna faded into view. She was vague and translucent. Equally ethereal Skitters grabbed her arms and dragged her from the cellar. I could hear nothing, but I could see she was screaming.

'Just think,' Midnight said as Anna and I watched in horror. 'You can save her from that. She can't remember it now, but it did happen. That's why she's here, why she's lost. You can stop it from ever taking place. And you get to save the world as well. Can't be bad, can it?'

I stared back at him, feeling empty and numb. Work for Midnight – work for a man who wanted to destroy everything I knew and loved. Or watch it all destroyed before me. Either way, really, the world was coming to an end.

'Bad?' I said. 'It's as bad as it gets.'

Midnight shrugged, as if it didn't matter to him either way. 'Let me know if you change your mind,' he said. 'Preston can't stop the bomb, so you've got ten seconds to decide.'

The countdown clicked over to 9.

Preston was frantically reaching inside the bomb casing. But the look on his face told me that Midnight was speaking the truth. Beside me, Anna's face was a mask of utter horror.

8 . . .

The Skitters were chittering away, giggling at us.

7 . . .

Midnight's laughter added to the unholy noise.

6 . . .

'Sorry, Anna,' I said.

5 . . .

And with Midnight's laughter echoing in my head, I hurled myself at the bomb.

4 . . .

I scrabbled and tore at the casing, shouldering Preston aside and thrusting my hand deep into the mechanism.

3 . . .

'No?' Midnight said. 'What a pity.'

2 . . .

Then he and the Skitters faded away. Leaving just the silence, and Preston and Anna and me.

1 . . .

And the bomb.

As it exploded.

'We don't have long,' I said. 'Midnight will soon realise there's a problem and be back.'

'What happened?' Preston said.

'Are we dead?' Anna asked.

'We will be, if I can't find a way of getting rid of the energy from the blast,' I told her. I reached into the bomb casing and pulled out the small glass sphere I'd stuffed inside when Midnight thought I was desperately trying to defuse it. The time synchronisation coordinator I'd taken after our previous encounter – in future America.

It was glowing brilliant yellow and was so hot I could barely hold it. I could tell, I could *feel*, what I had to do with the energy – how it worked, what would happen.

'The power of the blast,' Anna said, 'all captured inside there.'

'But if we don't use that power, and soon, it will escape anyway. The blast will happen, just a minute or so later than Midnight planned. It'll still rip apart reality.'

'What are you going to do?' Preston asked.

'I do have a plan,' I assured him. 'But you need to get away from here. Right away. Go home, quick as you can, and pretend none of this happened. Because,' I said as seriously as I could, 'none of it happened. I can make sure of that. But only once you're safe and away from here.'

'What about you?' he asked. 'And Anna?'

'We'll be fine. Really, fine. Go home and – I hope, I think – you'll find your daughter waiting for you there.'

Anna and Preston embraced briefly, then he left. All the way across the room and up the stairs he kept glancing back, as if he thought he might never see Anna again. I hoped he was wrong.

'You can do it?' Anna asked as soon as we were alone. 'You can put us back.'

'Yes,' I lied. 'I can put us back.'

'Both of us – there's enough energy for that?'

'Of course. But we have to be quick.' I could feel the power, the energy trying to escape from the little ball. Soon it would, unless I let it free. 'You first,' I said. 'I'll follow.'

Anna frowned. 'So – this is goodbye.'

I did my best to smile. 'Suppose it is, yeah. I won't forget you, Anna,' I promised.

'I won't forget you, Jamie.'

We hugged each other tight, just for a moment. The sphere was so hot now I almost dropped it. I could feel it beginning to crack under the enormous pressure of the energy trying to escape from inside. I didn't want to let go – either of the sphere or of Anna. I hoped she thought I was crying because it was goodbye, and because I was happy to be going home.

I wish.

I held out the little sphere, felt the power. A crack appeared in the side and I directed it at

Anna. I eased out as much energy as I needed to put her back into time, and to protect her for as long as possible. Which was all of it.

🕐 WEDNESDAY 5TH MARCH 1941

I think I'd always known it was possible, right from that air raid. It was one of the first times that Anna and I spent time just talking, after I was lost. I mean really lost. Once it was real and I understood what was happening.

She came here because it was where her parents lived. As close to them as she could get. She'd sit through the air raids while they were in the shelter in the garden and leave before they came back.

I sat with her that night – I could see myself and Anna through the window. The blackout curtains were drawn, of course, but there was the tiniest of gaps. Just enough for me to look through and see myself and Anna talking earnestly as the bombs fell around us and someone shouted for water to put out the fires.

When we left, after the all clear, Anna

mentioned that the people who lived there would be coming back inside. With their baby.

But how could they have a baby? Colin and Mary Preston never had a daughter – because Anna was lost.

But what if she wasn't. What if there was the *possibility* of a daughter after all. If something had happened to get time all muddled up and confused so that lost Anna did actually exist – maybe just for this one night. But she was there, she was real.

I watched myself come over to the window and peer out through the gap as Anna turned out the light inside. Maybe that night – I mean the first time I went to that night, with Anna – maybe I caught a glimpse of myself watching. Maybe I thought it was just a reflection. I can't be sure – after all, maybe it was.

But I wasn't looking for myself. I wanted to see the baby.

And now, back there once more, I turned away from the window and looked down the garden to where a much younger Colin Preston emerged from the half-buried metal hut. His young wife cautiously followed him, clutching her baby tight to keep her safe. Anna. Real Anna. Anna who had never been talking inside the house with me, because now she was back.

Anna – who I'd lied to. Perhaps that was the price of her existence . . .

🕐 SUNDAY 11TH SEPTEMBER 1955 (AGAIN)

The driver could tell there was something wrong as soon as he turned into the drive. He must have seen the other cars picked out in the headlights – big, black, official-looking cars – slewed to a halt outside the house.

He drove slowly and carefully, parking a short distance from the nearest of the cars before getting out. There were lights on at the front of the house, casting pools of yellow and white across the driveway. The cars had their headlights on too, throwing everything into a stark mixture of light and shadow. The driver stood for a moment looking round. It was Colin Preston.

He walked over to the main doorway and a

man in a suit came out to meet him. He was short and slightly podgy with thinning grey hair.

'Mr Preston?' he said.

Preston nodded. 'What's going on here?'

'My name is Blackler. I wonder if I could have a quick word.'

Together they walked to the side of the house, leaving room for the policemen who escorted Diane Chowdry out of the house and to the nearest car. The man I had known as Lewis stood in the doorway watching them, smoking a foul-smelling cigarette.

Gerald Chowdry was being brought out now. He looked white-faced with shock. Well, he'd just discovered his wife was a Soviet spy who'd been leaking all his department's innermost secrets to a Russian called Rasnitov. Enough to make anyone go pale.

They didn't know I was there, because essentially I wasn't. I watched from a split moment into the future. I was waiting for Mrs Preston to get out of the car and walk over to join her husband – asking him what was happening and if the dinner was off. Which it was.

The last person in the car got out too. It was a girl, who stood beside the car watching her parents. A police car turned in the drive, so the headlights were pointing straight at her. She had a slightly crooked, slightly nervous smile and was wearing a pale blouse and a loose skirt, both held tight at the waist by a big belt.

Anna.

One moment I wasn't there, the next I was. She didn't see me appear, it doesn't work like that. Maybe there was a ripple in the air, maybe it seemed as though I'd always been there, or emerged from the night. I don't know. But she looked at me curiously. Curious to know who I was and why I was there, not because she knew I shouldn't be.

'Hello, Anna,' I said.

There was something. A flicker in her eyes, unless it was the reflected light. But it lasted less than a part of a part of a second.

The worst thing, the very worst thing of all, was that her voice was exactly the same. So was the way she tilted her head slightly to one side

171

and sort of half smiled. 'I'm sorry,' she said, 'but do I know you?'

I forced myself to smile back at her. 'No, I'm sorry too. You don't know me. You never have. And you never will.'

She looked curious, but not surprised. A pretty girl who was spoken to by a strange boy. Nothing really that unusual. And I smiled, and I nodded, and I turned to the shadows and walked quickly away.

CHAPTER FOURTEEN

A police car passed me as I walked down the drive, away from the house. It looked square and boxy and old-fashioned. Not like the sleek, modern police cars that I was used to. I couldn't see inside, but I guessed Diane Chowdry was jammed in the back between two large officers.

The car stopped just before the end of the short drive, its lights cutting across the road beyond.

I don't mean it pulled up, or braked, or slowed to a halt. It just stopped. Like it had hit an invisible wall, only it didn't crash either.

It stopped because *everything* stopped. I watched the car for the briefest of moments, then turned quickly. I was hoping it was Anna. Hoping she'd be running towards me, clutching at her time dial and grinning. Ready to say, 'Only kidding' and be herself – the self I'd known – again.

But she was stopped too. Frozen by the car, silhouetted against the lights from the house as her mother walked back to her and her father continued to talk to the real Mr Blackler.

I turned back to the halted police car and Midnight was standing there. His cloak was billowing round him, although of course there could be no real breeze. It was the Skitters I could half see circling in and out. They stared at me through their nasty little red eyes.

Midnight wasn't looking too happy either. He slapped his black cane into his gloved hand as if it was a weapon. Well, it was.

'Hello,' I said. It sounded small and feeble and inadequate.

'Jamie Grant,' Midnight said. His voice was deep and dark and laden with anger and menace. 'You must think you're so clever.'

I shrugged. I didn't really trust myself to answer.

'Yet you're the one who's still lost. The boy who can save others, but never himself.'

'Better than destroying others,' I said. I was surprised how confident and defiant I sounded.

'The boy who *thinks* he can save others,' Midnight went on as if I had not spoken. 'Only when it comes down to it, he can actually save no one.' He smiled – a mirthless, unpleasant threat of a smile. 'That's why I'm here. Not to see you. That would be too easy. No, I've come to see her.'

He meant Anna. He must have been disappointed – I hoped he was disappointed – when I just turned and nodded in her direction. 'She's over there. You've seen her. Now go.'

The Skitters hissed and spat, sensing their master's anger.

'Oh no. She opposed me just as much as you did. Now someone has to pay for that.'

'And you think you're picking on the easy target?'

'You'd rather I destroyed you? Took you out of time for ever, so you're not just lost but totally non-existent? Dead?'

175

'I don't think you have that power,' I said calmly. And the strange thing was, I felt quite calm. I knew he was about to blow his top when he worked out what I'd done. But even so . . .

'You believe you've become strong enough to oppose me?'

'I've done it before.'

'You may have escaped my power before. But do you really think you can *defeat* me?'

'Not yet,' I told him truthfully. 'But my powers are increasing, and my abilities and my under-standing of how to use them.'

'Then perhaps I'd better destroy you now.' He thrust out his cane, pointing it straight at me. The air crackled with power, and then . . . nothing.

Midnight frowned.

'I've bought myself a bit of time,' I explained. 'The power of the blast was absorbed by the coordinator and I had to send it somewhere before the thing burned out.'

'You put Anna back into time,' he said slowly. He was working it out.

'And there was some power left over. Not

enough to put me back too. But enough to soak myself in the energy as I directed it at Anna. Enough to protect me, like a shield. You can't break through it. Time itself is keeping me safe.'

'It can't last for ever,' Midnight told me. He wasn't quite shouting, but it wasn't far off. 'That power won't last. It will fade and seep away. And one day, boy, you will be vulnerable.'

'You think so? Every day I get more powerful. Every day I'm better able to defend myself and oppose you. How many days can you afford to wait?'

I don't think he was even listening. He was looking past me – at Anna, standing by the car thirty metres away. I turned to look too, and I could see what he must be seeing. The pale aura that surrounded the otherwise ordinary girl. More than just the glow from the lights. Time itself, keeping her safe.

'Twenty years,' Midnight said quietly. 'That's all you've given her. Twenty years.'

'Twenty years, three months and nine days. Close enough. Before the energy seeps away.'

'And then she's mine – and make no mistake,

I'll be there. Just as soon as I can, I shall have my revenge.'

'Are you sure?' I looked him in the eye. 'That's twenty years in which I can get stronger. Twenty years I've got to prepare.'

Midnight laughed. He actually laughed at that. For the first time I felt cold inside – afraid and alone. I wanted – needed – Anna, and she was no longer there for me.

'Have you learned nothing?' Midnight said. His Skitters were laughing too, leathery faces screwed up into masks of amusement. 'Twenty years is only a moment away.'

He turned, the red lining of his cloak catching the light. Then it was gone, faded to nothing as he disappeared. But I knew where he was going.

🕐 Saturday 20th December 1975

Ever since then, I've felt as if my whole life has been moving towards this point. I've been further forward in time and back so far you wouldn't believe it. But I always knew that one day I would have to come to this time. I couldn't put it off, not for ever. Just hold it at bay and buy myself some . . . some time. Until I was ready.

But of course I'll never be ready. Not for this, not for now. I have done so much since that day outside the Chowdrys' house in 1955. Grown so much stronger. Had so many adventures and met so many people.

I know you don't remember me. I know you don't believe me. But it's all true, every word of it. I remember it as if it was yesterday – which maybe it was. Like I said, I lose track. I mean, it was all so long ago.

There was a time when we were friends. There was a time when, I think, you liked me. When we did so much together. We saved the world. But you can never remember, because for you – the you that lives here and now in the real world – it never happened.

I wish I could have left you in peace. I wish I didn't have to come here, and see you, and tell you all this. I thought you'd look so different, so much older. Yet really – to me – you look exactly the same as you always did. This is what Senex tried to warn me about – here and now. Because it's been twenty years and three months and nine days and you're not safe any more.

He's coming, and there's nothing I can do now, Anna. Except be here, with you.

CHAPTER FIFTEEN

He looked no more than about twelve, but the way he spoke seemed much older. The boy wasn't crying, not quite. His face was pale and he was watching her closely. Attentive for any reaction.

Anna Curtis leaned back in the chair, her tea left untouched on the table. 'It's quite a story,' she said. 'And yes, before I was married I was Anna Preston. But you do know it's just a story, don't you?'

The boy sighed and looked away. 'I'm sorry,' he said quietly.

'No, I'm sorry.' She stood up and started to tidy away the tea things. 'I shouldn't have asked you in. Did my son Mark put you up to this? Are you one of his friends from school?'

'You don't believe any of it, do you?' It sounded more like an accusation than an admission that he had made it all up.

Mrs Curtis picked up the tea tray. 'I never saw you before,' she said with forced patience. 'I never knew anyone called Jamie Grant. I have children of my own who are almost your age – I'm old enough to be your mother.'

The boy looked away, staring out through the net curtains to the street beyond. 'I can prove it to you,' he said.

'I doubt that.'

'All you have to do . . .' As he turned back, she saw that there were tears rolling down his cheeks. '. . . is wait. It's almost time.'

The clock on the mantelpiece began to chime the hour.

And stopped.

Outside, a car was motionless in the middle of the road. A young man balanced impossibly on a frozen bicycle. A bird was silhouetted against the grey of the cloudy sky.

Utter silence.

Broken by the smash of sound as Anna dropped the tray. Milk splashed across the carpet. A cup shattered. The teapot tipped over.

The boy waved his hand – a casual, unthinking gesture – and the tray was back on the table, the cup mended, the milk back in the jug. Just as it had been a few seconds earlier.

'I'm sorry,' he said. 'It's too late for stories. Too late for trust. Too late for anything.'

'It's all just – stopped.' She turned to him, her mouth open in astonishment. 'Like you said. Frozen. Time has . . . stood still.'

'Yes. He is coming.'

'Nothing is moving. Nothing at all.'

They both turned at the sound of the doorbell.

'Don't answer it.'

But the sound had broken the spell. It was just a story – a stupid story. A trick. Mrs Curtis hurried along the short hallway to the front door. Anything to get away from the mad boy and his wild stories. Anything to convince herself the world was normal – that *she* was normal.

'Please don't answer it.'

The front door was frosted glass. The person standing outside was a dark silhouette against the afternoon sun.

'Whatever you do, don't open the door!'

A tall figure, wearing a top hat and holding what might be a walking stick.

The boy was running after her.

'Don't open the door!'

There was movement through the glass – indistinct, blurred, flurries of movement like wings. Maybe a dwarfish, imp-like figure crouched beside the tall man.

'Anna – don't let him in!'

'Oh, Jamie,' she said, 'can't you see it's just a story?' And she reached for the door.

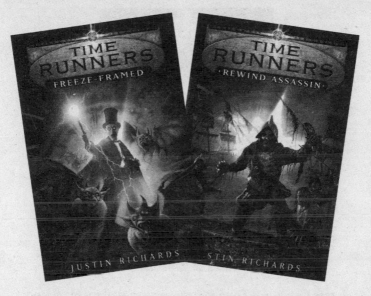

PAST FORWARD

ISBN: 9781416926443

Jamie Grant is a Time Runner – recruited by his friend
Anna to help fix problems with time. In the year 2021,
at a scientific compound outside Washington DC, chaos
has erupted. Someone is developing time travel – but
that shouldn't happen for centuries yet . . .

There's a terrifying monster on the loose and, somewhere,
their arch enemy Darkling Midnight is lurking. Can Jamie
and Anna find out the truth about the monster and reverse
the scientists' experiments before it's too late?

"An enjoyable read for all junior sci-fi fans."
Jill Murphy, thebookbag.com